RUST THE REJECTED

A WOLF SHIFTER REJECTED MATE PARANORMAL ROMANCE

BILLIONAIRE WOLVES SERIES
BOOK TWO

CHARMAINE LOUISE SHELTON

CONTENTS

WANT FREE BOOKS?

Want to know what happened to Jagger's best friend Dylan? Find out in *Dylan The Rogue: A Wolf Shifter Fated Mates Paranormal Romance* your FREE Book!

Click Cover Below or visit **bit.ly/ CLBooksDylanTheRogue** to subscribe to my newsletter for latest news and launches, books from my author friends, and sizzling reads in book promotions. Plus, start reading the steamy fated mates romance for bad boy wolf shifter Dylan.

Can I heal the tortured heart of my fated mate, even though she rejected me?

By day, I save patients in the ER. At night, I'm the doctor for my pack—the Billionaire Wolves of Miami. I work hard and play even harder. A wolf shifter whose busy life should fulfill my wants. Yet, I long for my fated mate. When a carefully concealed secret reveals her, Dr. Natalie Moore rejects me. A needle hurts. But this pain… Ouch.

As an OB-GYN, pregnant women may surround me all day, and I care for them. But that doesn't mean I want any parts of being pregnant or having pups! So, I suppress my wolf. No male will ever claim and mate me. Until an unfortunate accident brings Dr. Rust Ingolf sniffing around me. He may be sinfully sexy and tempt me. But. No.

And then, there's my old pack I ran away from. The leader wants me and will stop at nothing to make me his mate. How can I risk another?

*Their steamy love story is a standalone in the sizzling **Billionaire Wolves Series** of interconnecting stories featuring wolf shifter fated mates romance. Get a glimpse of their dynamism in other books.*

Anthem: "Never Gonna Give You Up" Rick Astley
https://www.youtube.com/watch?v=dQw4w9WgXcQ

Visit CharmaineLouiseBooks.com

 *ust*

"Oh, my, Dr. Ingolf. What a big stethoscope you have, Sir. So long and hard. Ooo and look! It even has a shiny tip. Shall I blow on it to warm it for you, Sir?"

The submissive purses her full, glossy lips as she stares up at me from the velvet pillow between my feet. A rich chocolate brown rims her dilated pupils.

But it's the sight of her creamy pillowy tits overflowing the cups of her pink lace corset that makes my cock leak pre-cum. The perfect size to fit in my large hands and soft. Nothing against silicone enhancements. But the feel of naturally lush tits with pinchable plump nipples wins hands down—or hands full.

My mouth salivates as much as my cock drips.

The Alpha Dom in me knows I should correct the sub's forward behavior. I did not command her to fist my dick—only to kneel. Any other time, I would toss her over my thighs and spank her round ass. The globes on either side of the skimpy lace thong would match its color for a delightful rosy shade. My palm itches for the punishment.

Instead, I sigh and pinch the bridge of my nose—not a nipple.

I've had back-to-back nights as a critical care surgeon at Miami's busiest hospital emergency room. The urban location has more than its share of acute, life-threatening injuries that require immediate surgery. Trained to perform well under pressure, I never hesitate to pick up the scalpel to save a patient.

My duties require the utmost focus. I cannot allow distractions. A patient's life—many times their heart—is in my hands, literally.

So, when I have a rare night off from the ER and no one in our pack needs Dr. Ingolf, I don't waste it. I take advantage of the opportunity to revel in my dominate proclivities.

A trip to Club Sol & Mani Miami provides a safe space for those in the BDSM lifestyle. The luxury, members-only club on Ocean Drive owned by the Miami Wolves Pack promises a night of pleasure.

I let my gaze return to the sub. She winks at me. Uh. No.

"Oh, naughty pet, how you misbehave," I tsk as I tuck my cock back into my bespoke trousers and zip up. Her mouth droops in dismay. "I must let the resident Dom know you like to top from the bottom."

Her glossy lips pout as elegantly shaped eyebrows pinch together and mar her pretty face. The little she-wolf even dares to growl at my reprimand.

Well, damn. That will never do.

She yelps as I scoop her from the pillow and over my muscular thighs. Long blonde hair falls over her face like a silky curtain. Her hands scrabble for the floor while her shapely legs flail.

I trap them with one of mine and press a hand between her shoulder blades to still her movements. A deep growl of my own halts her wiggling. Then a swat to her left ass cheek makes her jolt.

"Enough with this, naughty pet. You will take your punishment like a well-trained Club Sol & Mani sub. Twenty spanks, and you will count each one. Miss one, and we start anew. Do you understand?"

She shivers as I add Alpha power to my words. The musky scent of her arousal flares. I inhale deeply. My cock throbs, and my wolf howls. Yeah, it's been a while.

"Yes, Sir. I apologize and will behave appropriately."

I smirk as my palm rubs the soft skin of her upturned ass. A moan slips past her lips, and her pelvis tilts to push her ass into my hand.

THWACK.

"You disobey during a punishment?"

Her ass lowers as she shakes her head. Blonde strands sway with the light catching the golden streaks.

"Words, naughty pet. I will have your words."

"N—No, Sir."

"Count, or we start from one."

"One, Sir." She replies immediately.

Halfway through, the intoxicating scent of her arousal permeates the air in my private suite. A damp patch of it spreads through the wool of my trousers. I rim her slick pussy lips with the calloused tip of my middle finger.

She gasps, and her greedy core clenches. Then she wails when I issue three successive spanks to her swollen folds. But she doesn't miss the count.

I thrust two tapered fingers inside of her pussy. It pulsates around the digits, sucking them in deep. So tight and wet. I stifle a groan. Too damn long.

"Twenty, Sir."

The sub ends on a choked pant.

I lift her to straddle my lap.

Tears stream down her reddened cheeks. Like her ass, they bear a crimson shade. I pull the Ferragamo silk pocket square from my suit jacket and dab her face. Chocolate brown eyes now softened lower to stare at my chest submissively.

"You did well, pet. Now, you will think twice before topping a Dom. Won't you?" I ask with a cocked eyebrow.

"Thank you, Sir. Yes, I will," she whispers.

"Good. Now, we fuck," I say as my hands cup her heated ass, and I rise. Quick strides take me to the sex swing. Even quicker, I strap her in.

Excitement shines in her eyes, even as she keeps them

lowered. Her teeth nibble at the corner of her lip. Dainty fingers wrap around the black suede straps. Her thighs—slick with her juices—quiver in anticipation.

She doesn't have long to wait.

I unzip my trousers, and my aching cock springs free. It slaps back against my shirt. The engorged mushroom tip reaches my belly button.belly button.

Teeth marks dimple her lip as she moans at the sight of my well-endowed dick.

I fist its wide base and stroke up the veiny shaft once, squeezing below the head. Pearly beads of pre-cum drip to tile floor. Her lust-filled eyes follow their descent. I slip a condom over my cock. Her eyes snap to my face when I grab her hips and pull.

The sex swing arcs forward. We watch as her pussy swallows the length and girth of my cock. The tip parts her glistening folds, then disappears inch by delicious inch into her soaked core. When my heavy balls meet her heated ass cheeks, we groan in unison.

My eyes close. The sensation of tight, wet warmth clamping on my dick makes my balls tingle. Finally. Fuuuck. I relish the moment before I withdraw to my tip.

The sub mewls in protest at the loss.

"Oh, little pet, I will satisfy you many times over. But you will not cum until I give you permission. Do you understand?"

"Yes, Sir, thank you, Sir!"

I chuckle wickedly and pull the sex swing forward to plunge back in. With each arc of the swing, her pussy flutters around my cock. Too much and I draw back, edging her until she begs my permission to cum.

The forceful thrusts pop her tits from the corset. I lean over and suckle the plump nipples. She moans as her inner walls clench around my cock. A few more thrusts, and my control hangs on by a thread.

"Now, pet! Keep cumming until I give you permission to stop," I growl.

She keens as her first orgasm causes her body to buck in the sex swing.

I grunt and growl as I fuck her through one wave after the other of her toe-curling orgasms until she's limp in the swing. Then I chase my release with a roar to the ceiling. My knees turn to jelly, and my still erect cock slips from her pussy.

She whimpers.

I slip the condom off and toss it in the discreet trash can. She watches with hooded eyes as I tuck my junk away, then uncuff her from the sex swing and carry her to the bed. With a sated sigh, she rolls to her side, curled up like a well-fed pup. I chuckle to myself as I head to the en suite bathroom for a warm, moistened cloth and clean her gently. I apply a soothing salve to her warm crimson ass cheeks, and she moans softly. Tucked beneath the silk sheets, I leave the contented she-wolf with a note beside her pillow to stay the night and enjoy breakfast.

I skip the shower and go downstairs to my McLaren P1 LM. The ride to my beachfront penthouse on Ocean Drive

—where most pack bachelors live—brings me back to reality.

I let my mind wander as I drive along Collins Avenue, South Beach. And as my thoughts have in recent months, they go to what I long for to complete my life. No matter how successful I am in the ER or how many—or how few —nights at Club Sol & Mani, one thing still eludes me.

My fated mate…

"Hey, Big Red, you finally made it. Got held up in a storage closet by a hot nurse checking your vitals?"

"The Love Doctor is available for private appointments —one or multiple patients per session. Leave your name and number after the beep."

I growl in response to the jabs and guffaws of my best friends—Dylan Vang and Jagger Larson—as I enter the Wolf Den on Moon Island.

The hangout spot for the males on our pack's private island set in Biscayne Bay—the body of water behind the barrier island of Miami Beach across from South Beach. The Wolf Den offers every luxury amenity and boys' toys imaginable to entertain the males. A gym, steam room, sauna, bowling alley, game room, cinema, wet bars, and more allow us to relax in our true nature. No concern humans hear us growl when we lose. Or growl at Jagger and Dylan…

"Fuck off, losers. A human kid fell off a bike and fractured her arm right before my shift ended. A higher priority than shooting pool with you two," I say as I select a cue stick from the wall rack. "Her olecranon took the brunt of the impact while the lateral epicondyle of her humerus suffered distal fracture—"

"Okay, Doc, we don't need to hear your nerdy description of a broken arm. Get a drink and rack the balls already," Dylan says, rolling his amber eyes to the ceiling. "We're trying to have some fun here, you know."

Jagger chuckles and claps me on the back as he strides to the wet bar.

"Rack the balls. What'll you have to drink?"

I nod my thanks and ask for two fingers of aquavit—a nod to our Scandinavian Viking roots. Wolf shifters have a high tolerance for alcohol. It's not getting drunk for us. Rather, we enjoy the taste.

"D., you want a refill?" Jagger asks, then takes Dylan's old fashioned glass when he nods.

While I gather the billiard balls on the sand-colored felt of the modern desert pine pool table, Dylan sets the music playlist. I glance around the game room at the other males. Some play poker, laughing about a joke across the room. Four play pool at another table. A few gather around the wet bar watching a Miami Heat versus LA Lakers basketball game.

"Viggo and Tag can't make it tonight. Viggo had an emergency at one of his clubs, and Tag was too mysterious about his reason to bow out," Jagger says about our other best friends as he hands us tumblers.

He's our pack's Alpha in a long line of leaders of the *Billionaire Wolves of Miami*—as the other packs refer to us. With good reason, since we're the most powerful pack in the South. Several millennia ago, Scandinavian Viking wolf shifters sailed from the Old World and landed along the East Coast of what's now the United States. The six packs moved throughout the continent to form territories, with ours settling here.

Jagger continued the Larsons as our pack Alphas, despite Dylan's misguided challenge. Fortunately, the two reconciled recently. We've been best friends since we were pups. Now in our late twenties—except for Viggo, who's twenty-six—we can enjoy our friendship for decades to come. Including tonight, and it's the distraction I need.

The three of us play a few rounds of pool as we rib each other and talk about work. Aside from being the Alpha, Jagger serves as the CEO of Larson Enterprises, Inc. It's the source of our pack's wealth with its luxury hotels, fine dining, clubs, and lounges throughout our territory across the south. Dylan made his billions with an early investment and spends his time competing in an underground fight club in New York City.

Viggo and Tag work with Larson Enterprises as President of Clubs and Lounges and COO and are Jagger's younger brother and beta, respectively. Dylan and I chose to work outside of the company.

My need to be a doctor driven by wanting to care for our pack and the horrible memory of a male driven to madness because he never mated. A flash of the vision of him running wild as his wolf attacking other members in the Everglades—where our pack has a camp compound—makes me shudder. I hit the billiards ball at the wrong angle. It skips past the corner pocket and bounces off the top rail. Lost in thought, I barely hear Jagger.

"Damn, Rust! What are you aiming at? *My* balls?"

Dylan throws his head back and roars in laughter. Others turn to our table and grin at his infectious guffaw.

"Not the Larson family's jewels. The gods forbid!"

Jagger's ice blue eyes narrow at Dylan, who wipes tears from his eyes.

"You're a regular comedian, D. These jewels already sired fraternal twin pups with my gorgeous fated mate, Sage. And she would *not* appreciate any damage to my extraordinary package," Jagger says with a smirk.

I laugh. But inside, an ache stabs my heart.

After all these years, Jagger and Dylan found their fated mates—even with Dylan not believing in the concept. The lucky bastard claimed a beautiful Russian she-wolf. Jagger's Sage is the stunning and powerful High Witch of the Coven of the South turned she-wolf and our pack's Luna. Now, she wields never-before-seen magick because of his DNA mixing with hers. I delivered their twins despite Jagger's growling because a male was near his fated mate, especially being up close and personal with her most private areas. It's part of my responsibility to our pack regardless of the males' possessiveness of their mates, fated or otherwise.

I believe wholeheartedly in fated mates. Yet, I haven't

found mine. Each year I get older, and the fear of the madness affliction striking me grows stronger. Meanwhile, two of my best friends enjoy the bliss of a fated mate bond. Damn.

"Yeah, well, my jewels filled my beauty with a pup," Dylan responds, then turns to me. "And you better not fuck up when it's time for her birth. I damn sure wish we had a female doctor. I don't want your eyes and your hands anywhere near my Sasha."

I shrug and say, "The she-wolves I care for do not differ from any other patient. I have no further interest than to help them with their medical requirements."

Dylan huffs and sips his aquavit, eyeing me over the rim of his glass. Then he pulls his mobile from his jeans pocket. A grin spreads across his face, and his amber eyes gleam as they scan the screen. His fingers fly across it as he types.

"Well, fellas, it's been a pleasure. But I gotta go. My fated mate requests mint chocolate chip ice cream, and I vowed to give her all her heart's desires. And then some!"

He claps Jagger and me on the back and strides towards the door.

Jagger's mobile rings. Undoubtedly, it's from his fated mate, based on the giant grin as he answers the call. With a not so genuine sorry to end our evening early, he gives me a salute and heads out the door.

I shake my head and glance around, trying to decide if I'll join the other males for poker or to just hang out. Instead, I finish my drink and go to my Bugatti La Voiture Noire. Another boys' toy, and the most expensive supercar in the world. Since I don't have a fated mate to lavish with "all her heart's desires," I might as well spend my money on the finer things for myself.

Once again, the ride back to my bachelor's penthouse leaves me yearning for the one who will complete me.

My fated mate…

 atalie

"Dr. Moore, your next patient arrived. Shall I bring her to examination room two now?"

So engrossed in the patient's medical chart on my desk, I startle at my nurse Thandie Ross' question. I glance up to find her standing in the doorway of my office.

"Oh! I didn't mean to scare you, Dr. Moore!" She says as her sepia cheeks redden apologetically.

I wave off her concern and shake my head.

"Not a problem, Thandie. I was caught up in her case. It's intriguing. Right in line with my specialty of critical care. Kindly take her to the exam room," I say, then arch an eyebrow. "And remember to call me Natalie unless we're with patients. I'm not into formalities."

She smiles and leaves.

I close my eyes and sit back in the chair. My mind drifts to my former pack out west and the drive for me to care for females who require the close attention and knowledge required for dangerous pregnancies.

"Amanda, you don't look too good. Your face is pale, and your breathing is labored. Are you sure you want to continue our walk? I think we should head back," I say as we reach the tree line surrounding our pack's land. "We already walked a mile, and I don't think we should go any further."

My older sister takes another step forward, then winces as she gasps and clutches her round belly.

I grab her arm to prevent her from falling. My gaze scans the area for a comfortable spot she can rest. A fallen Douglas fir catches my eye.

"This way. You can rest over there, then we're heading back. And do not argue, Amanda. I'll get the midwife to check on you."

Amanda nods as she grinds her teeth. Slowly, we make our way to the evergreen, where I help her sit gingerly. She closes her eyes and inhales, then exhales. The grimace disappears as she settles.

"Listen to me, Nat, no matter what happens, you take care of yourself. Don't let anyone force you to mate. We're not meant to be breeders. Dad would never allow this to happen if he were still alive and Alpha."

Tears sting my eyes, and I glance away. It won't due to upset Amanda—not now with her in distress. But she's right. Had our parents not died with so many other members of our pack from the unexpected affliction two years ago, Sam would never be Alpha or mated to Amanda. He defeated the other males, then took Amanda as his mate since she's the eldest daughter of the prior Alpha. I thanked the gods I'm four years younger at sixteen.

We sit in silence—lost in thoughts—until Amanda moans. She glances down at her lap, then up at me. The grimace returns as her onyx eyes—so like mine—widen.

"M—My water broke... Nat," she pants.

I turn towards the closest building. It's too far for Amanda to walk. She'll never make it.

"I'm going to shift and run to the midwife. We'll return with Sam and his pickup truck to bring you home. Don't follow me, Amanda, please!"

She nods as she sucks in a ragged breath.

I kiss her forehead—covered in a sheen of sweat—and step back to remove my clothes. I allow my body to relax and accept my wolf to take over. My other half lives on the fringes of my being. Always ready to spring forth at my call, then retreat at my will. An ability born of our kind so long ago and marks us different from full humans.

The sensations of my bones reshaping and muscles lengthening to shift me from my human form to that of my wolf block out all else. Crackling and a flash find me on all four paws within moments. My wolf appears with midnight fur and a white streak like my widow's peak.

I cast a quick glance at Amanda. Certain she's not moving, I dart away. My paws pound the grassy terrain as the salty air from the Puget Sound wafts past my nose. It's a rare sunny morning with no sign of rain. Nothing to impede my race to the midwife and Sam. Thank the gods!

I run straight to the older she-wolf's home. My howl as I approach brings her to the front porch. One glimpse at me, and she rushes inside. She returns with her bag and a dress.

"Here, Natalie, shift and change. Where's Amanda?" She says as she hands the dress to me. "Hurry, she hasn't looked good to me in days!"

My wolf retreats, and I pull the dress over my head as I tell her about Amanda. We hurry to get Sam from the Alpha's office. He's with his beta and a few other males. They leer at me as we enter. I ignore them and focus on Sam.

"Amanda's in labor! We need you to bring her back home with your pickup—"

"Why the hell did she go anywhere when I told her to stay her ass at home?! She never listens, no matter how many lessons I give that stubborn she-wolf."

My mouth gapes. Does he mean he hurts my sister? Why didn't she tell me?

"Shut your mouth and take me to her."

I blink at his harsh words but set the thoughts aside. My sister and the pup come first. We'll have time to figure out what to do about Sam after the birth.

We drive to spot and find Amanda on the ground with her back against the evergreen and her sweatpants beside the tree. Her knees bent with her feet wide apart on the grass. Her face contorts as she screams in agony.

"No time to take her back. I'll deliver the pup here. Natalie, you've watched me enough times to know what to do," the

midwife says as she hurries to Amanda's side with me close behind her.

My sister doesn't register our presence until the midwife kneels in front of her and calls her name. Amanda opens her eyes and stares unseeingly. Another contraction hits, and she wails how much it hurts. Blood gushes to the grass.

The midwife checks her, then glances at me. Regret fills her brown eyes as she shakes her head.

Tears blur my vision. I grab Amanda's hand and whisper how much I love her, along with words of encouragement.

Sam growls.

"You better not die on me, Amanda! Deliver my pup and quit with your whining. You hear me? Of course, it hurts. Who the hell said it would be easy?"

Tears—not just from the pain in her womb, but from the heartless words of her mate and our Alpha—stream down my sister's flushed cheeks. Her entire pregnancy was rife with pain. Not one moment was idyllic for her. She did her best to ignore it. But I could tell by the sadness in her eyes she was not enjoying her pregnancy. And the oaf of a male wolf shifter she mated with was of zero use to her.

Like the other males in our pack, he only cares about his offspring. Their sole focus on increasing our numbers since so many of the pack died from the unexplainable affliction. Now, instead of cherishing the she-wolves, the males view us as breeders. And the gods forbid if a she-wolf fails to produce pups or ages out of fertility! She's tossed aside by her mate, and he chooses another. She becomes the head mate while the original moves to the sidelines and hopes he will provide for her, too.

The day my sister and her male pup died in childbirth marked the end for me. Instead of mourning his loss, our Alpha turned from their lifeless bodies to pin me with his intense stare.

"You will become my mate since your sister failed me."

That night after I buried my sister and her pup beside the graves of our parents, I left the only home I'd ever known.

I gathered some clothes and my savings—including the sizable inheritance from my parents. Without a backward glance, I left my pack's land. After years of witnessing the pain and the loss she-wolves experienced—even before the years prior to the affliction—I knew the gods wanted me to help females as an OB-GYN. It became my mission through the years at the University of New Mexico under-grad and medical school to excel in my studies. During my residency, I applied to positions far away from my former pack. Miami accepted me.

My eyes open with a fierce determination to help my patient and her unborn baby. As I have for the last twelve years, I use the tragic memory of my sister and her pup to urge me to do my utmost to care for other females. From finishing my studies early and succeeding in my residency until now, I do it all to honor my sister and the struggles of the she-wolves of my former pack.

I take a deep breath and exhale to clear my mind. Focused and determined, I leave my office for the examination room. Ready for the day's challenges.

"Natalie, Thandie and I are going for happy hour with a

few others in the department. Do you want to join us? You'll get to meet more people and have fun doing it!"

Paloma Sabela Garcia—the OB-GYN department secretary—smiles at me as Thandie nods in agreement.

I consider their offer, then decline.

"Thanks ladies. But I'll have to take a raincheck. Too many boxes sit in my living room waiting for me to unpack them," I say, then grin. "You have no idea how many times I rotated three wrap dresses this week!"

They glance at each other, then burst out laughing. With a shrug, I join them.

It'll be nice to have girlfriends again. During school, I was too busy to bond with others. Without the pressure to do well and to finish early, I have time to spend with others. Just not tonight.

I watch them still giggling as they leave my suite of rooms.

After I complete notes in the charts for the day's patients, I head to my car. Fortunately, work study, scholarships, and grants covered most my education. So, I splurged on the pre-owned Volkswagen Beetle convertible. Now, I can enjoy the sunny Miami weather every chance I get. So, unlike the rainy Pacific Northwest. And I'll do anything to distance myself from that place.

As soon as the ignition starts, I press the button to lower the roof. Then pull my mane of midnight hair with its snow-white widow's peak into a ponytail and slip on a pair of oversized glamour girl sunglasses. The playlist of

Miami-inspired dance music has me tapping my fingers on the steering wheel as I navigate through the streets.

I stop by the spot famous for its Cuban sandwich Paloma Sabela recommended. My mouth waters at the delicious aroma of ham, roasted pork, salami, and fresh-baked bread. At the checkout, the cashier suggests the Materva Cuban soda. I thank him and head to my car, more than ready to chow down.

It's a quick ride to my furnished, one-bedroom rental apartment. I chose a spot near the hospital for quick access in case I need to deliver a baby, or the mom may need help with little warning. The less time lost, the better in the cases of my critical care patients.

As I open the front door, my heart sinks. Box after giant box stretches from the middle of the living room to the two windows on the opposite wall. A few sit open with medical books, lingerie, or shoes spilling out. The side of one wardrobe box labeled dresses gapes open—items on hangers visible. I unpacked the ones marked for the bathroom for my toiletries and cosmetics last week.

And of course, I opened the most precious box that contains my special serum. A quick check revealed the glass vials and syringes remained intact. I couldn't fly with them. Too much of a risk should the TSA choose to confiscate the box or to question the serum's purpose.

I shudder at the thought of humans learning about wolf shifters' existence. Worse yet, they gain the knowledge I can't even share with my own kind. My formula and its purpose would cause an uproar in the entire shifter community. Its impact goes beyond wolves.

With a shake of my head, I put the thoughts aside and head to the eat-in-kitchen. A tiny mosaic-topped café table with two chairs sits in a corner by the window with a view of the park across the street. I set the bags of food and sodas on the countertop, then wind my way past the boxes for the bedroom.

It's not large. But the room fits a queen-size bed with nightstands on the wall opposite the door and a small, three-drawer dresser beneath the window. I can see the same view of the park as the living room and kitchen while I sit in bed.

I strip and let my hair down on my way to the bathroom on the other side of the bed. A quick shower helps wash away the day before I eat dinner. My stomach rumbles just thinking about the tantalizing Cuban sandwich. Yum!

Bundled up in a comfy robe and my hair up in a drying turban, I settle at the café table. My mouth waters at the delicious aroma of the meats blended with Swiss cheese, pickles, and spicy mustard. The sandwich is so large, I'll save the other half for lunch tomorrow.

My leg swings as I eat. Laughter bubbles up at the memory of my mother teasing me about being so greedy I'd swing one leg and hum in delight as I ate. The flash of her smiling face brings me a moment of joy before the sadness tries to creep in. Once again, I shake my head to dispel the negativity.

It's a fresh start, Nat. Don't dwell on the past, I chastise myself.

As I wash the dishes, the alarm on my mobile chimes with the ringtone for Creedence Clearwater Revival's "Bad Moon Rising." Hurriedly, I dry my hands as I grumble trouble will definitely be on the way if I don't inject my serum as scheduled.

From the time I left my former pack, I knew I needed to avoid all shifters. I had no desire to encounter them. Distance from the paranormal world prompted me to research a method to suppress my wolf. Various combinations of regular human medicines and trials finally resulted in a serum that hid my wolf, even from me. No scent detectable. Not a chance of a shift. The only downside is the loss of my enhanced healing and senses, including my ability to detect a shifter. But I'm free of my wolf with no way for others to find me. Safe to be me and to live my life as I choose—not forced to mate and breed. Just as Amanda told me.

Unless I didn't inject the serum on time each month. Then I would revert to a wolf shifter over a period of time. To test the amount of time I had before the reversion to my wolf, I skipped a scheduled dose. Each day, an element of my wolf appeared. By the seventh day, she returned fully. Without hesitation, I injected the serum. In two days, it banished that side of me again.

I do not know the side effects of the combined medications other than as they stand alone. However, the risk outweighs any negative result. It's been three years, and I have no regrets.

As an OB-GYN, pregnant women may surround me all day, and I care for them. But that doesn't mean I want any parts of being pregnant or having pups!

So, I turn off the alarm, slip my mobile in the robe pocket, and stride purposefully towards my bedroom. As I pass through the living room, I pick up the stepladder. Even at five feet, nine inches, I'll need the extra height to reach the rear corner of the top shelf in the closet where I put the box.

Atop the ladder, I collect the box in one hand while the other keeps my balance. As my foot lowers to the next step, the robe's belt snags on the corner of the ladder. I pull the belt loose, but the ladder teeters precariously. My heart clenches as in what seems like slow motion the ladder topples sideways, my fingers reach and miss the closet door, and I free fall to the tile floor. Eyes widen in horror as my precious box flies from my hand, arcs through the air, and crashes to the floor. The shattering of bone and glass followed by a wail echo in my ears.

Pain radiates along my arm. But it doesn't compare to the agony in my heart. The shattered remnants of the vials represent the last of my serum supply. An entire six months destroyed in seconds. Tears fill my eyes.

And now, I regret the loss of my wolf. My arm hurts like hell. I can't drive in this condition. Drawing on my strength and determination, I slip my mobile from the robe pocket and dial 911.

CHAPTER 3

ust

"DR. INGOLF, I hate to do this to you since your shift ends in a few minutes. But the EMTs brought in a doctor from the hospital who fell off a stepladder at home. X-rays reveal multiple upper arm fractures. She's in area five."

I curtail the flash of annoyance and replace it with a smile as I accept the patient folder from the ER nurse. It's not his fault, nor can I blame the patient. They have nothing to do with me on duty for almost twelve hours and mere minutes away from being off shift.

"Duty calls," I respond, saluting him with the folder, then stride towards the curtained area. Scanning the images, I wince at the type of fractures the patient sustained. Damn.

"Hello, I—"

My mouth drops at the luscious swell of an exposed breast. The more-than-a-handful—even for my sizable ones—mound peeks from behind a drab gray hospital gown. The opening reveals a heart-shaped birthmark on the inner curve of her breast. My eyes slide to the imprint of a plump nipple outlined against the thin cotton. My mouth salivates. Unconsciously, I lick my lips.

"Oooooo…"

The pitiful moan—not the kind I prefer to hear from a female—snaps me out of the unprofessional lust fog.

Dammit, Rust! What the fuck?!

I shake my head. Obviously, I need another night at Club Sol & Mani if I'm getting horny over a hurt patient…

"Hello, I'm Dr. Ingolf, Dr. Moore," I say, to continue my disrupted introduction. "Let's get a look at your arm. Shall we?"

Her eyelids flutter open and the most soulful eyes I've ever seen peer at me. Air rushes from my lungs at the intensity of her onyx orbs—even while full of anguish.

Unconsciously, I rub my chest.

"P—Please… The pain."

The nurse steps around me and raises a questioning eyebrow at me. I return my gaze to Dr. Moore.

"On a scale of one to five, how much pain—"

"Eight!"

"How well do you tolerate morphine, Dr. Moore?"

Her eyes close as she considers my question. Then she

mutters under her breath and pins me with a fiery glare. Lightning flashes in the onyx depths.

"I've never had it. But give it to me. I'm a doctor, for goodness sake! I'll prescribe it to myself if I have to! Ooooo…"

Her eyes squeeze shut as she sags against the upraised bed.

The nurse stifles a laugh at her snippy command and glances at me for approval.

My inner Alpha Dom bristles at her bratty behavior. But I ignore it since she's in pain—and not the erotic kind. I give the nurse a nod to administer the medicine via IV drip, and he leaves the curtained area. I hold back the fact a doctor cannot self-prescribe a controlled substance to themselves in the state of Florida. No need to upset her further.

Instead, I stride to the X-ray reader on the wall and place the images on the glass surface, then flick on the light.

"Well, *Dr.* Moore, the nurse will administer the morphine. Meanwhile, I'll explain the fracture to you and the next steps."

Her eyes open, then narrow at the images. A gasp escapes her mouth as she scans the breaks in her arm bones. For a moment, her in-charge demeanor drops, replaced by a small, sad female.

My heart goes out to her. The urge to comfort coming from out of nowhere.

"You had a nasty fall. I'm sure it must shock you even as

a doctor. But it'll be all right, Natalie. I'll help you," I say as I offer her a comforting smile.

Her head jerks up to bring her gaze to where I tower over her at six feet, six inches. Gone is the vulnerability. Onyx daggers hurtle towards me as she sits up straight. Only a flicker of pain appears before she shutters her eyes.

"I do not need your *help*, Doctor Ingolf. Your medical attention to my arm will suffice. So, get on with it," she snaps. The curtain draws back, and the nurse steps through. His eyes dart between the two of us. She shifts her gaze to him, and her eyes drop to the morphine bag in his hand. Relief floods her face. "Thank you, nurse. There's one step in my treatment."

Well, fuck me.

My inner Alpha Dom gives me a dour face, and my wolf flicks his tail. Fine, two can play this game…

"Dr. Moore, I will reset the bones and place your arm in a soft cast to allow room for swelling. You will return tomorrow for a fiberglass cast worn during the healing period—typically twelve weeks. More than likely, you will require physical therapy to regain proper use of the limb. The option to see an orthopedist to further your care lies with you. Do you understand?"

She blinks at my dominance. I catch a glimpse of submissive behavior as her eyes lower in deference with a nod.

"Words, Dr. Moore. I will have your verbal response."

This time, her mouth gapes as her eyes jump to my face. She studies me a moment. Emotions war in their dark depths—surprise, reluctance, confusion, finally irritation. Her chin lifts in the air. She scoffs.

"*Yes*, Dr. Ingolf."

My cock twitches of its own accord. I do my best to ignore the instant desire to punish her for continued bratty behavior.

An erotic vision of her torso braced against the bed, hospital gown flipped over her back, bare ass exposed, and her feet spread wide emerges in my mind. My palm itches to spank her soundly. It lands on the fleshy portion of a round globe with a resounding THWACK. A warm crimson shade blooms around my hand as I hold the heat in. She tosses her mane of ink black hair with a swath of white and cries out in wild abandon as her arousal flares. A succession of spanks lifts her to dance on tiptoe. She pants as aromatic slick slides down her inner thighs from her dripping pink pussy to puddle on the floor—

"Dr. Ingolf?"

Damn! Not again, Rust.

I shake my head to dispel the highly inappropriate vision, then turn to the nurse. I shift on my feet to adjust my burgeoning erection down my inner thigh. Thank fuck the white coat hides my cock. I use the patient file as an additional shield in front of my crotch. Then school my face despite the heat on my cheeks and clear my throat.

"Pardon. What did you say?"

In my periphery, Dr. Moore tilts her head as she inspects me. Onyx eyes narrow. Full lips purse.

The nurse eyes me, too. But he doesn't comment on my

lack of attention. Instead, he tips his chin towards the IV pole.

"I administered the morphine drip. Her pain level on a scale of one to ten dropped to a four. She's ready for you to reset the bones. I can get the supplies you need."

"Excellent, thank you," I respond and turn to the patient—*not your fantasy lover, Rust.* "Dr. Moore, we will proceed…"

*N*ATALIE

D*R*. I*NGOLF RILES ME*.

"I'm sure it must shock you even as a doctor… I'll help you."

"Do you understand?"

"Words, Dr. Moore. I will have your verbal response."

Who the hell does he think he is?! So condescending! I'm not some damsel in distress who needs a knight to ride up on his steed to save her from a horrible plight. Well, sort of. But that's beside the point!

I'm a doctor. His equal. He owes me respect. The same he would afford a male doctor in my place. Not make me feel small and dependent upon the heroic Dr. Ingolf!

Males. They always put themselves above females. Think they know better for us than we do for ourselves. Speak to us in any manner they choose. Expect us to bow down to them. Controlling so and so Dr. Ingolf!

And no, his dazzling golden-flecked hazel eyes do not make my heart flutter in the least. Nor do my fingers flex to remove the hair tie and tangle in his thick, shoulder-length hair the color of dark ginger. His innate air of command does absolutely nothing for my nether bits.

All I experience is annoyance added to my pain.

"Ooooo!"

His hands pause as he realigns the bones in my arm. Even with the morphine drip direct in my vein, the movement of the fractured bones proves excruciating. No matter the tenderness with which Dr. Ingolf handles my arm, it still aches. Badly.

My enhanced wolf healing ability spoiled me. In all my youth of racing up steep mountainsides, leaping over felled trees in the forest, and charging across open fields, not one scrape or sprain set me back. Within hours, I healed completely. Even the scars faded to nothing. And I was off for another romp with my friends. Blissfully unaware of the amount of suffering my body could experience without my enhanced nature.

"Are you still with me, Dr. Moore?"

My eyes peek open at the sound of Dr. Ingolf's smooth baritone voice. *Those* eyes scan my face to gauge my discomfort. I whimper. Lost for a moment in their depths, I stare, no longer mindful of my disdain for the male. Until he opens his mouth again...

"The morphine only dulls the pain so much. Of course, it hurts. It's not easy."

Gah!

I growl low in my throat as my eyes narrow on him. I want to gnash my teeth. On his arm! Damn the male for sounding just like Sam! Unbelievable. Obnoxious. Rude. Oaf!

The descriptions roll nonstop in my mind as I grind my molars to prevent another whimper from my mouth. I will not give the good doctor any satisfaction of witnessing my torture, only for him to say something patronizing. Bedside manner, my ass.

I won't even close my eyes. Instead, my gaze flits about the curtained area as I tune into my surroundings. A baby cries to my right. Its father's murmurs of loving words reach my ears. Across from me, a human male in his late thirties holds his head between his hands. The nurse beside him asks questions about his motorcycle accident. A doctor walks past, trailed by interns. A female answers her question with confidence. While a scowl forms on a male's face. I roll my eyes in disgust. Gah!

"I realigned the bones. Next step in your treatment, the placement of the posterior long arm splint."

Without glancing at Dr. Ingolf, I nod and continue my observations of the busy ER. Out of the corner of my eye, I notice a slight smirk on his handsome face. Masculine with angular bone structure yet with soft, full, kissable lips. WHAT?!?!?!

It has to be the morphine kicking in for real now. The drug robbing me of all sensibility and restraint. I bite back a curse. The gods help me!

Fortunately, a commotion at the entrance to the ER

distracts me. Three nurses rush past my curtained area while an EMT shouts for help. A female's cries mingle with the calls for a doctor STAT.

Dr. Ingolf's hands pause as they adjust the last strap on the splint. He cocks his head as though listening to something. His nostrils flare. A glow appears in his hazel eyes. He turns to the nurse.

"The incoming patient requires my expertise—"

"Let me guess, your gut instinct tells you?" Dr. Ingolf nods in response, and the nurse continues. "A lot of patients owe their lives to your gut instinct, doctor."

"True. And Dr. Moore is stable. You can put the sling in place and discharge her pain meds and a list of the orthopedic doctors," he says hurriedly. He glances at me, nods, and rushes towards the new patient.

At last, he's gone.

But why the hell do I feel at a loss?

Get a grip, Nat. What is this? Emergency Room Stockholm Syndrome, or what?

I barely listen as the nurse speaks to me. Carefully, he places the sling over my head to rest at my neck and loops it around the soft cast. A few adjustments, and I'm all set.

When he asks if I have someone who can take me home, I shake my head and yawn. The morphine and the late hour make me sleepy. He tells me to wait a bit, and I settle against the bed. My eyes shut.

"—still here? Did something happen after I left her with you?"

"No, Dr. Ingolf. She doesn't have anyone to take her

home. I didn't want her to go alone, considering she only came in with a robe on. Plus, she's a hospital doctor. I felt responsible for her safety. I'm leaving now and can offer her a ride home."

"No, I'll do it. I left so abruptly, I owe it to her to check in."

My fuzzy mind absorbs the conversation on the other side of the drawn curtain. But I can't believe Dr. Ingolf just offered to drive me home. I should protest. However, I don't want to get in a rideshare with only my robe and the hospital socks. It has to be after midnight by now.

As my hand slides across the sheet in search of my mobile, the curtain parts. Dr. Ingolf strides in.

"Hello again, Dr. Moore. The nurse tells me you adjusted well to the splint. How do you feel after some rest?"

"H—Hello," I say with a dry mouth, then swallow to try again. "Hello, Dr. Ingolf. Fine, thank you. And I'll accept your offer of a ride home. I'm not inclined to take a rideshare at the moment. If you give me a second, I'll be ready to go. Oh, and thank you."

The little smirk appears on *those* lips again.

I ignore it and wiggle my way to the edge of the bed. Immediately, he reaches out to grasp my good arm. But I wave him off. Let's not go overboard with accepting his help.

He inclines his head and steps away. The curtain falls back in place.

Once again, a twinge of loss gnaws at me. I berate

myself as I slip the hospital gown off and replace it with the robe. One arm through the sleeve and the other side draped over my shoulder. I tighten the belt. A glance down at my feet, and I shrug. I'll just have to make do with the socks and watch out for sharp objects.

A rumbling chuckle meets my ears as I step from the curtained area.

With a hip leaned against the nurse's station, Dr. Ingolf laughs with a young brunette. She bats her long eyelashes at him as her hand reaches to slap his forearm coyly. Their heads dip. His mouth goes to her ear. She covers her mouth with a dainty hand and giggles. She. Giggles. Typical male doctor, female nurse flirtation. Gah!

Just what I needed to witness to eliminate any ridiculous stirrings of attraction towards *Dr.* Ingolf. With a smirk of my own, I step forward.

"Ready," I say loudly.

CHAPTER 4

atalie

"Thank you and enjoy your day."

I smile at the hospital dispensary pharmacist and pivot, only to bounce off a solid wall. A white coat over a pair of green scrubs blocks me. Hands steady me. Who the hell?

My head snaps back and up, up, up to find Dr. Ingolf staring at me questioningly. His hazel gaze flits from me to the pharmacist and lands on the bag in my hand before returning to my face.

I tighten my grip on my medicines as my lip curls defensively. Then I think about it and relax my features, offering him a cordial smile. No need to set off alarms with him regarding the contents of my bag.

Two days passed since my fall and the first I've been

able to leave my apartment for the hospital. The ride home with Dr. Ingolf proved challenging.

He insisted upon carrying me from the ER to his SUV. *I don't want you stepping on glass and cutting your foot, Dr. Moore. And you don't want additional hours in the ER unnecessarily, do you?* So much bigger than me and dominant, I had no choice but to let him have his way.

At the SUV, he placed me on the passenger seat and put the safety belt across my chest. I bit my lower lip when his knuckles grazed the curve of my breast. Instantly, the nipple beaded at his unintentional touch. He maintained a straight face. But I swore his eyes glowed. When he shut the passenger door, I moved as close to it as possible without plastering myself to the rich wood inlay. Being naked beneath my robe disinclined me from getting too close to him.

However, his masculine scent engulfed me—citrusy, musky, and spicy. Tempting. I let the window down and used the excuse of needing fresh air after all the time in the ER. He nodded with a slight smirk. I stared out the window and did my best to ignore the sexual attraction.

He stuck to generic questions about where I was from, how long I'd been at the hospital, did I like Miami so far. I skipped over details to my past and stuck with my college and med school period through the present. Very easy and detached conversation. Just what I preferred.

Once we arrived at my apartment building, he climbed out of the SUV and jogged around its front to open my door. With a firm grip around my waist and under my thighs, he hoisted me from the seat. For a second, our eyes connected. I was lost. Again. Fortunately, the spell broke when he asked me to push the door shut. The soft thud reminded me to squash any intention beyond doctor-patient care. All the better!

Despite my protest I could make it to my apartment from the lobby, he ignored me and strode to the elevators. With a scowl, I pressed the call button and the floor button once inside. Not wanting to add to the intimate connection of me being held bridal style in the confines of the elevator, my gaze glued to the floor indicator.

His warm breath tickled the top of my head. I ignored it. But the strong pulse of his heart against my breast caused tingles to zing throughout my body. The temptation to snuggle against him almost won. Fortunately, the doors slid open, and he strode into the hallway.

At my front door, I typed the code onto the electronic lock panel and pushed the handle. He stepped inside and glanced around. A frown marred his handsome face at the sight of the boxes. I gave up protesting at being carried and simply pointed to the bedroom door. He settled me on the bed and left for the kitchen. A bottle of water on the nightstand and instructions to take the pain medication every eight hours as needed and to keep my arm dry and elevated were his last words.

When I heard the door shut, I used the app on my mobile to activate the lock. With a sigh, I snuggled against the fluffy pillow—not Dr. Ingolf's solid muscular body.

Unlike now.

"Dr. Moore, good to see you getting about. I notice you wear the fiberglass cast. How's your arm?"

My cordial smile widens—more in relief he didn't call me out for the odd mixture of medicines he must have overhead me requesting based on his questioning reaction.

"Better, thank you, Dr. Ingolf. I just left the orthopedist. If we were in high school, I'd ask you to sign my cast," I respond with a grin. "Instead, I'll thank you again. You impressed her with your realignment of the fractured bones. As you said, twelve weeks should mend my arm."

His hazel eyes dance as he returns my grin. The overhead lights catch the shimmering golden flecks.

"Good to hear I know what I'm doing after all! Even better, you're well. I couldn't help but observe the boxes in your living room. Let me know if you want help to unpack, especially with your arm—"

He reaches into the pocket of his white coat and withdraws a pager. His eyebrows knit as he scans the screen. A hand rakes through his loose hair.

"Listen, I gotta go. You know where to reach me, *Dr. Moore*," he says as he rushes off.

I watch him jog down the corridor. His dark ginger hair and the white coat fly. Long muscular legs carry him away with ease. He's at least a foot taller than anyone else. So, it's easy to follow his path through the patients and the hospital staff. A few nurses stop to ogle him. My returned enhanced hearing picks up their comments.

"Dr. Ingolf is by far the hottest doctor in the hospital!"

"I wish I were his emergency..."

"What I wouldn't give for Dr. Ingolf to give me some tender loving care. Talk about a steamy bedside manner!"

A couple of them giggle behind their hands like starstruck fangirls.

Gah!

I shake my head, then pivot and stride in the opposite direction. I'm not due back in the office until the day after tomorrow. Which is perfect since I still need a few more medicines to complete my serum formula. The pharmacist expects the order to arrive that day or the next one. I just have to lie low in my apartment. The last thing I need is to come across a wolf shifter. Unconsciously, my feet hurry towards the exit as I clutch my precious cargo to my chest.

I make it home with no incident after I pick up Thai food for lunch. A glance around at the loads of boxes and I just might take him up on his offer to help. I make my way to the bedroom and store my medicine supply on a lower shelf in the closet—less risk of another mishap. Then change into my robe and settle on the sofa to binge on food and Netflix.

But my mind drifts to Dr. Ingolf. I searched for him on the hospital website. What else can I do all day with a bum arm? My curiosity revealed more about the good doctor. Rust suits him with his dark ginger hair. A rich shade that sets off his golden-flecked hazel eyes as he stares at the camera in his bio photo. Those clean-shaven, chiseled cheekbones and square jaw give him a strong masculine appearance. The full lips curve in a slight smirk to provide a glimpse into his confidence. Combined with his degrees from Vanderbilt University, published works, and multiple accolades, those in need of his expertise as a critical care surgeon can rest assured, they're in excellent hands.

Large hands with tapered fingers. Skillful hands. Hands I can imagine on more than just my arm.

The television screen fades as I focus on a revised version of Rust driving me home from the hospital.

His eyes flick between me and the road ahead as he weaves through traffic. I squirm in the seat to ease the carnal ache in my core. The lustful glint in his amber eyes shines in the light from intermittent streetlamps through the windshield. The corner of his full lips quirks up at my breathy moan.

A hand lowers to my thigh. Naughty fingers slip beneath my robe. The tips seek my swollen clit nestled within my folds, already slick with arousal. On a needy moan, my legs spread, giving them better access.

The thumb pad circles the sensitive nubbin, applying more pressure with each pass. My hips rotate in sync with its erotic rhythm. Moans and musk fill the interior of the SUV. Long fingers breech my folds. My pussy walls clench around them, drawing them deeper into my greedy channel. I drop my head against the headrest and arch my back as the orgasm dances closer.

A sharp pinch to my clit, and my thighs slam together, trapping his skillful hand as I buck against it. It's so intense, I damn near levitate. Stars flash behind my closed eyelids while my mouth opens in a silent scream.

As the ripples dwindle, I sag limp against the seat, thigh muscles slack, heart pounding. My breath comes out in warm pants. A cloud of condensation ebbs and recedes on the window. Eyes flutter closed.

"Such a good girl," Rust croons as he pats my pussy, then licks my juices from his fingers.

The television reappears as the fantasy fades. I blink, disoriented. Reality returns.

I growl and take a forceful bite of food.

Do *not* go there, Nat!

To open myself up to dating leads to love, then either or both parties wanting a committed relationship. One that leads to marriage, then to the male making demands of the female. He controls what she does with her life and her body. Forces the female to put her desires aside for his wants, including children, whether or not she wants them. Her health matters little as long as she produces.

Sam and Amanda—along with other mates in my former pack—are prime examples of that destructive relationship. The anguish he forced my sister to deal with breaks my heart. Her death and her pup's stillbirth finish any relationship I could ever want, even before it starts.

Sure, our father wasn't as extreme as Sam and his cohorts. But Dad persuaded Mom to mate with him despite them not being a fated pair. He was older and—as I learned later—didn't want to endure the madness unmated males experience after a certain time without a mate. He also wanted an heir to replace him as Alpha. They tried many times for male pups, resulting in my Mom's decline in health. A situation exacerbated by the unexpected affliction years later. So, once again, his needs supplanted my Mom's life.

I swipe tears from my eyes and reaffirm I want no parts of a male in my life, being pregnant, or having pups.

Not happening! Not now, not ever. And most especially not with *Rust Dr. McDreamy Ingolf*!

CHAPTER 5

atalie

"I HAVE a date with a guy my sister's husband knows. They work together at the firm. She swears the guy's cute and nice. Not at all like the one she hooked me up with the last time..."

"This had to be the longest day ever! I cannot wait to get out of this waist trainer. Hourglass figure be damned!"

"Yes, sweetheart, Mommy will be home soon... No, you can't eat cookies before dinner..."

"Let's grab a drink after work..."

My palms press against my ears to lessen the banter from everyone around me. All. The. Way. In. My. Office. With. The. Door. Shut.

Gah!

Another day ushers in the return or improvement of a

wolf sense. Some good, some not so great. Less pain in my arm and more shoulder mobility allows me to cover my ears. The healing process speeds up—though not quite as fast as during my full shifter days.

Two days ago, my wolf hearing restored. Also, not fully. I picked up the comments about Dr. Ingolf in the corridor easily—the level low. But now, the conservations around my office bombard my brain. A constant buzz I can't avoid. Not to mention the everyday sounds of doors closing, the clicks of high heels on the tile floor, papers rustling. They're all amplified, especially since it's been years since I had powerful hearing. It'll take a period of adjustment to reacclimate. In the meantime, I'll pick up ear plugs…

A less invasive buzzing in my white coat pocket draws my attention from completing notes in the day's patient files. I'm surprised Paloma Sabela didn't ring my office landline instead of paging me. But the message isn't from the department secretary. I grab my mobile and dial the number quickly.

"Hello, this is Dr. Moore. What's going on?"

"Dr. Moore, are you still at the hospital?" The ER nurse asks, then continues when I confirm. "Thank goodness! We need you in the ER STAT. A pregnant woman arrived with a knife wound to her abdomen…"

I fling the door open and race down the corridor as I listen to the details. Thandie steps from an exam room, and I yell I'm needed in the ER. She nods and rushes to the OB-GYN reception area to alert the staff. I end the call before stepping onto the elevator. My eyes close as I gather myself to prepare for a delicate case. Those around me disappear as I turn inwards and focus on my breathing.

The computer-generated voice announces the ground floor as the doors ding open. I rush out as I exclaim ER emergency and bypass the other passengers. My feet fly. I reach the ER and rush towards the operating room. The nurse waves me over and helps me scrub for surgery in the OR anteroom. I remove the sling from the damn cast to maneuver my arm as best I can. I ignore the slight twinge of pain. Patient first.

"Dr. Moore here. Give me an update," I announce as I stride through the door held open by the nurse.

Beeps from the machinery indicate a weak but steady heartbeat and an erratic one. My eyes go to the female patient. Tatters of her bloodied clothing lie on the floor. The metallic odor of fresh blood invades my nose. Her eyes remain closed in a pale face. An intubation tube protrudes from her mouth to assist with her breathing. The size of her belly puts her in the third trimester. I pray to the gods the knife missed the baby, and it's developed enough to withstand an emergency C-section. The mother, we'll see.

"Dr. Moore."

My eyes jerk to my left at the sound of Dr. Ingolf's baritone voice. Only his hazel eyes and his brawny frame offer distinguishing characteristics as the surgical cap, mask, and visor obscure his face.

"I stabilized the woman as best as I can, given the location and the severity of the knife wound. So, you'll have to work quickly to save the baby…"

As the lead surgeon, he goes on to update me while I check the baby's vitals. Thirty minutes later, I deliver the baby and close the C-section incisions. The knife nicked the little girl's shoulder and narrowly missed her head. The pediatric surgeon takes over the baby's care while Dr. Ingolf tends to the mother. I standby in case he needs help.

His skill level amazes me as he works swiftly to repair the damage inflicted by the knife. At times, his hands blur with movement. His intense focus serves the patient well. Not even a leaking abdominal aorta frazzles him. Less than half an hour later, the nurse rolls the mother from the operating room. She'll live to love her baby. Dr. Ingolf turns to me and smiles.

And damn if my heart doesn't flutter. A radiance about him after a successful surgery highlights the gold in his eyes. They glow internally. Enthralling me.

"You impress me, Dr. Moore," he says as he strides towards me. An air of confidence and masculine swagger exude from his being. Again, nurses peek at him behind their visors. But his eyes remain glued to me.

He leans over and his hand reaches out. My heart skips a beat as I gasp. He stifles a chuckle and inclines his head to the right of me.

"After you, Dr. Moore."

I glance over my shoulder to find his hand on the OR door. Color floods my cheeks as I lower my head and mutter a curse. For a moment, I thought he was reaching out to touch me. Get it together, Nat!

This time, he laughs out loud.

My head snaps up to find his hazel eyes twinkling.

"I think you got it together, Dr. Moore. I'm sure the mother will appreciate you saving her unborn child."

My cheeks burn as my gaze drops to his feet—enormous feet. How the hell did I speak aloud?! And why am I acting like those nurses?! But worse because I. Don't. Want. Him.

I nod and pivot, ducking beneath his muscular arm to hasten into the anteroom. He follows me to the biohazard bin and hamper. I avert my eyes as he removes the bloodied apron and the surgical gown. Briefly I imagine he strips to nothing but smooth skin and chiseled muscles, then beckons me. With a shake of my head, I toss my soiled garments in the appropriate place. Last warning, Natalie.

Determined not to make a further fool of myself, I remain silent as we move to the sink. Elbow to elbow, we wash our hands. Dr. Ingolf says nothing. But I sense he watches me out of the corner of his eye. Hurriedly, I dry my hands and turn to leave.

Others around us exchange words as they move about the anteroom. Their relief is palpable. I smile at them, also thankful we saved the mother and her baby. The anesthesiologist catches my eye. He saunters over.

"Dr. Moore, you did a phenomenal job with the baby. Smart and decisive. Are you done with your shift? A few of us are going for drinks. I'd love for you to come."

I detect the rapid beat of his heart. He's too eager for me to join him, which only means he wants more than I'm willing to give. No point in encouraging him. I open my mouth to respond when a muscular arm brushes against me.

"Actually, Dr. Moore and I have plans."

I glance up to find Dr. Ingolf towering over both of us. With a nod, he places a hand on my lower back and guides me towards the double doors. I offer a smile to the anesthesiologist. He stares mouth agape.

Out of earshot, Dr. Ingolf says, "I sensed you didn't want to go with him but didn't know how to decline without seeming distant. You can thank me for the save by having dinner with me."

I tilt my head back, surprised at his demand. The corner of his mouth curves in a smirk as his eyes glint with mischief. I can't help but to laugh at his gutsy move.

"Oh, you're good, Dr. Ingolf. Maybe too good. But I didn't want to join him, and I am hungry. So, I'll accept your demand to thank you over dinner."

He chuckles, then raises his hand. A black strip of cloth dangles from his fingertips.

Dylan

SHE FROWNS at the cloth and shrugs a shoulder.

"Your cast sling."

Her onyx eyes widen as her mouth opens on a gasp. Color suffuses her cheeks.

The scent of her distress confuses me as much as her ability to move her arm with such ease mere days after her fall. I didn't want to distract her during the surgeries by asking about it. Rather, I explained it as her running on adrenaline, more concerned about the patients than her own wellbeing. However, I find it odd she left the strap on the counter.

"You've been using your arm despite the fractures."

Her face shutters as she reaches up to take the sling. As she places it around her neck and slips her arm through it, she responds in a clipped manner.

"Yes, obviously, Dr. Ingolf. I find it more important to focus on my patient's life than to worry about a bit of pain I experience. I do not appreciate you questioning me. Good night, Dr. Ingolf."

She spins on her heel and marches off.

My eyes narrow as I scent the air. She's holding back on the full truth. And I want to know why.

"Dr. Moore, my apologies for coming across as nosy. That was not my intent. Your rapid recovery surprises me. As a medical professional, I'm sure you must understand," I say when I catch up to her. Her pace slows, and I take advantage. "But you can't tell me good night until after dinner. That's ill form for a debt owed."

She swings her head around and scoffs. Her waist-long ponytail slaps me in the mouth better than her dainty hand ever could. A smile tugs at the corners of her lush mouth. Then a giggle bursts from between her lips. She raises a hand and covers her mouth.

"How apropos, Dr. Ingolf. Hopefully, that'll teach you to open your mouth unnecessarily."

I chuckle wickedly and lean down to whisper in her ear.

"Were we in another place, *Dr. Moore*, I would show you exactly what I do with a long ponytail."

She jerks back as she sucks in a ragged breath. Her pupils dilate to pure black. Cheeks redden a deep rose I'd love to see on her ass from my palm. A vision of my cock buried within the complete O of her mouth leads to a barely audible rumble in my chest.

Her eyes widen to inky pools.

For a moment, I wonder if she heard the sound, or if it's her response to my filthy words. Fuck unprofessional. This female drives me feral.

Again, I take advantage of her delay and place a hand on her lower back. She doesn't pull away as I guide her through the busy ER. I check out of my shift and head towards the exit. I don't trust she'll follow me once in her car. So, I stride towards my Range Rover P530 First Edition (LWB). The luxury SUV serves as my preferred ride for hospital duty. Fully loaded, but not one of my flashy supercars. I press the key fob, and the headlights illuminate the area as the engine purrs to life.

"Hold on. I have my car. I'll follow you," Dr. Moore says as her heels dig in. "It's just over there."

I tsk, and her elegantly arched eyebrows draw together.

"You may think I'm a nosy SOB. But I assure you, I am a gentleman. We will drive to the restaurant in my Rover. After, I'll bring you to your car and follow you home to ensure you arrive safely," I say in a tone that brooks no room for debate.

She lowers her eyes as her teeth tug on her lower lip. My cock twitches at another show of her reluctant submissiveness. Better still at the delicious vision of those teeth grazing my thick shaft to my plum tip before her tongue laps pre-cum from my slit. Oh, the things I would do with the feisty female. Her gaze lifts to mine.

"Fine."

I nod and move forward. Inwardly, my Alpha Dom smirks, and my wolf's tongue lolls out hungrily.

"After a complicated surgery, I'm famished, and one spot always satisfies my needs," I say as my eyes flick from the road to Dr. Moore. Her onyx orbs shine in the darkened interior of the SUV as she stares back at me. Their glow surprises me. As I open my mouth to comment, she speaks.

"And what spot would that be, Dr. Ingolf?"

I blink and return my gaze to the road ahead as the traffic light changes from red to green. The niggle in the back of my mind dissipates with the flow of cars.

"Ah, yes, Prime 112. A traditional steakhouse with a modern touch and contemporary menu known as one of the best in the world," I say, then glance at her. "Do you eat meat?"

She stifles a giggle and nods.

"I do and could use a tasty cut. My appetite for beef increased recently," she responds with an enigmatic smile. Her fingertips reach for the console touchscreen, and she tilts her head. "Do you mind if we play some music? It soothes me post-surgery."

I agree, thinking I could help her with that even better. She scrolls through the satellite stations until she selects one, then sits back, eyes closed, effectively ending the conversation.

When we arrive at the restaurant, the valet helps her from the SUV as I round the front. She thanks him with a warm smile. For a second, I wish she offered the beatific expression to me. As though sensing my thoughts, she shifts her gaze to mine, and her smile widens. Fuck if my heart doesn't stutter. I ignore it and place my hand on the small of her back, guiding her to the restaurant's doors.

"Dr. Ingolf! What a lovely surprise."

The host steps from behind the podium and extends his hand in greeting. We shake, and I introduce him to Dr. Moore. He double kisses her cheeks, then leaves us to get my usual table ready. It's a prime spot within the kitchen, affording the opportunity to watch the chef and her team prepare tantalizing dishes.

I guide Dr. Moore to the bar to wait for the host's return. She glances around, and I see the space through her eyes.

Typical of a top-tier steakhouse, it features customary dark wood and exposed-brick walls. But it stands apart for its sleek and superb design with white leather and low lighting resulting in a sexy decor. Up-tempo music in the background makes for a lively vibe. An eclectic mix of ritzy patrons mingle at the bar and dine at the tables. With business casual attire expected some of the clientele raise eyebrows at our scrubs. But I could give a fuck.

I pull out a Lucite and white leather high chair for Dr. Moore. She smiles graciously as she perches on the seat. I sit beside her and signal the bartender. She comes over, and we order drinks. I raise my tumbler of aquavit.

"Here's to saving lives and to new relationships."

She frowns as her lips part, then shakes her head and raises her mojito.

"Cheers, Dr. Ingolf."

I cock an eyebrow and place a hand on her forearm to stop her sip.

"Don't you think we're on a first-name basis now?"

Once again, her onyx eyes glint in the dimness as that mysterious smile tips her lush lips. She slips her arm from beneath my hand and brings the glass to her mouth. The tip of her little pink tongue moistens the rim before she sips.

My cock throbs, intrigued by the erotic move.

"Yes, *Rust.*"

Fuck. Me. Or. What.

ust

THE FULL MOON above casts shadows from the towering pine trees onto the ground as I pad through the dense undergrowth. A barred owl hoots perched on a bough. I glance up. It spreads its wings and leaps into the air. The predator soars before it swoops down. A rustling in a bush and a shriek followed by silence indicate it found its evening meal. The metallic scent of fresh blood fills my nostrils. They flare as I inhale, savoring the aroma.

My turn.

Deep in the Everglades, I hunt.

I trot ahead, careful not to disturb the twigs and rocks beneath my paws. My eyes scan the surrounding thicket. Ears swivel to capture even the most subtle sound. My head swings to the right at a low snarl. The moonlight glints in a Florida panther's eyes. Hidden in the scrub, it watches me. I issue a challenging growl as I stand my ground.

Nearly twice the size of a regular wolf, I have no fear of the night's new predator. Thick red fur covers my massive body. Vicious fangs dripping with saliva appear as my lip curls. I snap my teeth as hackles raise. Paws stamp the ground. Another ferocious growl, and the panther turns tail with a disgruntled hiss. It slinks away further into the underbrush. I watch its retreat still alert should it circle back. Satisfied it's gone for good, I prowl on in search of my evening meal.

Animals detect the presence of an apex predator and scurry from my path. I bide my time and lope along. I allow my wolf to decide our route, using his enhanced sense of smell as a guide. My nose twitches as it catches hints of a hare nestled in its form, a few white-tailed deer gathered beneath a pine tree, and rodents in their tunnels. I don't have an appetite for them tonight. We move on.

The pine flatlands give way to a marsh. The roots of coastal mangroves provide cover for West Indian manatees and leatherback turtles. I push through the sawgrass, searching the still water for any signs of alligators. I have no desire to tangle with one, especially alone without my pack.

None seen—although they can lurk beneath the surface —I approach the water cautiously. Eyes dart about as I lower my snout for a refreshing drink. A few laps and ripples appear on the moonlit surface. I jump back just as the might jaws gape open where my head bent low to the water. A growl rumbles from my chest as the alligator slithers back beneath the surface. Yellow eyes stare until the water engulfs its giant head. With a last glance, I trot back to the tree line far from the water's edge.

My ears prick up at snuffling beyond a fallen evergreen tree. I lift my head to scent the air. A feral boar! Just the challenge I seek for my meal.

Well aware of their dangerous tusks, I give it a wide berth before I move closer. Remaining downwind to avoid it detecting my scent, I pad towards its rear. Also, out for its evening meal, the large boar lowers its head to use its tusks to forage for underground roots. Distracted, it doesn't notice me stalk, then pounce on its back. My canines sink into its neck as my claws dig into its flanks. Blood fills my mouth.

It squeals and bucks. I cling to it and shake my head, embedding my sharp teeth deep into its thick neck. Coarse hair pokes inside my mouth. But I refuse to let go. Snarls match its squeals. It drops to the side in an attempt to dislodge me. I use my back feet to clamber up. My unyielding grip ensures the feral boar rises with me.

My teeth meet its spine. I give my head a final jerk. The vertebrae snap. The boar collapses to the ground with a grunt. I loosen my hold and sit on my haunches panting from the effort to down the beast. My head goes back, and I issue a triumphant howl.

Sated, I find a stream to clean my fur and to rinse my

mouth. As I shake remnants of water from my fur, my wolf whimpers. I glance around and find nothing of concern. A breeze blows across my fur like a lover's caress. My body shudders with instant carnal desire.

The touch of wind carries a scent I was born smelling the moment I took my first breath as a newborn pup. Earth, ferns, and fir trees mix with a hint of vanilla carried on the cool ocean breeze. The unique scent of my fated mate.

At last!

My heart races as I prowl in a slow circle to target her unique scent's direction. The low whine of my wolf increases to a joyful bark when the scent grows stronger further into the pine flat lands. I set off at a brisk trot.

Small animals scurry from my path. But they have nothing to fear. I'm on the hunt for my fated mate. She will receive my bite, not them.

Her unique scent beckons me with a wispy curl leading from her to my nose. The closer I approach, the stronger the pull.

My cock thickens and lengthens to the point of pain. Seed drips from the bulbous tip. The serum to lodge my scent beneath her skin to mark her as mine permanently coats my canines. My body prepares to claim my fated mate.

Up ahead, my keen eyesight spots a flash of white amongst a cluster of dense pine trees. The moonlight reflects off the fur. As I draw closer, her entire body comes into view. A gorgeous, sleek she-wolf with midnight fur on her body and a white streak on her head. Unaware of my presence, she continues to dig, then to drag fallen boughs to cover the spot.

My wolf howls just as I detect more than earth, fern, and fir trees mixed with a hint of vanilla. A musky aroma fills my nostrils. My fated mate is in heat!

I bound into the small clearing beneath the pine trees where she prepares her nest. Her head jerks in my direction. A whine greets me as she backs away, frightened by my sudden appearance. I rumble deep in my chest to soothe her.

Instead, her body tenses. Dark eyes dart around the space, seeking an escape. Before she can move a muscle, I block her with my much larger body. She bares her teeth with a snarl. I return a dominating growl and stand taller. She bows her head and drops to her back. Vulnerable belly and throat bared to me.

I nuzzle her with my snout. Gone is the growl replaced by the soothing rumble. She acquiesces with a soft whine. I nudge her flank for her to rise. She rolls to her paws and watches me with her head lowered. I prowl around her in a circle. The rumble in my chest remains constant. She stands still. I breathe in her unique scent, mixed with the musk of her heat. Once again, I nuzzle her body—neck, flank, base of tail.

My mind reels. After all these years of aching for my fated mate and fear of succumbing to madness if I didn't find her, she stands before me, ready for me to claim and breed her. Thank the gods. My wolf howls in agreement.

With a possessive growl, I rise onto my hind legs and wrap my front ones around her waist and back legs. My thighs bracket hers.

She lifts her tail.

So, ready to breach my fated mate, I plunge my cock deep inside of her. She whimpers and paws the ground with her front feet. My feral growls fill the balmy night air as I pump my hips forcibly. Her slick eases my brutal strokes. As my heavy balls draw up, I open my mouth wide. The serum drips from my canines onto her midnight fur. The drops shine in the moonlight like a bull's-eye for my mark.

With a savage growl, I lower my mouth at the juncture where her neck meets her shoulder. I clamp down, piercing her flesh. She howls and wriggles. My front legs tighten around her waist as I grind my jaw to deepen my claiming bite.

The base of my cock expands to form my knot. Her pussy contracts as she whimpers from the painful stretch. We lock together. Molten heat explodes from my cock to fill her womb with my seed. I throw my head back and howl to the moon above. She joins me for a carnal song.

During the fifteen minutes my knot ties us together, I rumble in my chest to soothe her as she quakes beneath me. Once my knot deflates, we separate. I lick where my claiming bite left blood on her fur, then her snout. She returns my affection with licks to my head and flank before she limps to the nest. I follow close behind.

She curls up on the boughs, and I lie beside her. As my

eyes drift closed, a chirping interrupts my slumber. I glance around for the bird with its incessant sound. An irritated growl pours from my mouth.

My hand flings out for my nightstand to stop the morning alarm from my mobile. Then my eyes snap open. I jump up to a sitting position and swivel my head.

Gone are the pine trees and the moonlit clearing beneath them. Instead of a nest made of boughs, tangled sweat-dampened sheets cover my legs. Fresh creamy jizz coats my cock, eight-pack abs, and pecs. Worse yet, my beautiful fated mate isn't curled up beside me, sleepy from my claiming. Aside from me, the king-size bed sits empty. And cold.

What the fuck?!

My damp palms press against my eyelids to clear my head. But the mobile continues to chirp. With an angry growl, I grab the mobile and jab the off button. I toss it onto the bed and throw myself against the pillows. My fists punch the mattress. I roar in frustration.

Only a wet dream. What a fucking tease!

NATALIE

"Oooh, *GODS!!!*"

My back bows from the bed as my fingernails claw the sheets and my heels dig into the mattress. An orgasm so intense I lose my vision and my breath as it barrels through me. My body convulses as I fall back to the soaked sheets. My pussy pulsates with delicious aftershocks. A warm puddle of my arousal lies under my ass.

I open my eyes, panting. My blurry gaze skitters around, expecting to see the giant red wolf amongst unfamiliar pine trees. Instead, my bedroom comes into focus. I cover my sweaty face with shaky hands. A moan slips past my lips as I taste his fur on my tongue, smell his wild musk.

It felt so real. His groin pounding against my rump, driving his ginormous cock deep into my tight pussy. The stretch and burn of his knot. The searing pain of his claiming—

My head snaps up as I touch the spot on my neck where he bit me. Relief washes over me. Nothing there. Even though an ache in the area makes me wince. I shake my head. It wasn't real. Only a dream. Well, nightmare.

"Natalie! You have to get the rest of the medicines. It's your wolf warning you."

I chide myself aloud as I roll from the bed and limp towards the bathroom.

Fuck if I don't feel his cock still inside of me. My pussy clenches at the thought. I growl and yank the glass shower door open. The warm water soothes the aches in my body. But does nothing for the turmoil in my mind.

Tomorrow marks seven days since I dropped the serum to suppress my wolf. And obviously, she's ready to merge with me completely.

But not if I can help it.

On the ride to the hospital, I begin to unwind as the sun warms my skin and the balmy breeze flows over me. At a red traffic light, I tilt my head back and close my eyes to revel in the Miami weather. My enhanced hearing alerts me to the movement of cars way ahead of mine. I take a moment to inhale deeply, then open my eyes on a slow exhalation. My increased sense of smell hasn't returned yet. But I can detect the salt carried in from the Atlantic Ocean. Such a contrast to the coolness of the Pacific Northwest. And I love it!

Before I head to the OB-GYN department, I pick up coffee and a toasted corn muffin with butter from the hospital's cafeteria. It buzzes with activity. Visitors and staff mill about the glass-enclosed counters to select food and beverages or line up at the checkout. Beside a wall of floor-to-ceiling windows, people sit at tables. Beyond the windows, the view of the interior garden with its colorful flowers and palm trees brings a touch a pleasantness to a place often filled with sadness. I cast a last glance at nature's beauty and stroll towards the registers.

On my way to the elevators, I spot Dr. Ingolf—I mean *Rust*—striding towards the cafeteria. He's so damn handsome. His long, dark ginger hair is loose and glints in the overhead lights. Hazel eyes twinkle as he laughs. Full, kissable lips curve upwards. Broad shoulders fill out his white coat. Even beneath the basic scrubs, the flexing of his muscular thighs appears. Thick thighs save lives. And strong enough to—

Cut it, Nat! That erotic dream has you ramped up. Still.

I shake my head to displace lustful thoughts of the good doctor. With a clear head, I glance back in his direction. He's nearly at the cafeteria doors.

Just as I'm about to raise my hand to catch his attention, I notice a female doctor at his elbow. He leans over and whispers in her ear. A flush blooms on her copper skin as her brown eyes twinkle. She tilts her face up and smiles at him. He smirks as he pushes the door open and steps back to allow her to walk in ahead of him. His eyes follow her. Then he enters the cafeteria, and the door closes.

GAH!

Jealousy surges through me faster than a brushfire of dry timber. My eyes narrow as my lips purse. A feral growl slips past them. My free hand forms a fist. I want to tear off this stupid cast and fling it at the happy couple. Wild-eyed and snarling, my wolf claws beneath my skin, eager to shred the female to pieces. The level of violence shocks me.

Air! I need fresh air!

I pivot on my heel and rush towards the hospital exit. I battle to restrain my wolf. Never has she behaved wildly uncontrollable. She remains on the fringes of my being and only comes forth when I summon her, then retreats as I bid.

My breath comes in shallow pants. The bustle in the lobby rings in my ears. I cover them and lower my head as my pace increases. I burst through the doors and jog around the corner. My eyes close and chin drops to my heaving chest. I bend my knees and slide down the wall. A tear slips past my eyelashes. Then sobs rack my body.

Gods, how I wish I could have a relationship with a male. Despite my bravado, I secretly yearn for a partner. Someone who cares for me and treats me with respect. Who loves me above all others. Wolves are not meant to be loners. We belong in a pack.

But it's just so fucked up how life treated me. My former pack's mentality damaged me. Ruined me for any possibility of a relationship. My wounded heart aches.

A light tap on my shoulder jolts me.

I lift my tear-filled eyes to find a human male asking if I'm okay. I nod and wave him off.

But I'm not. And it's the fault of my wolf!

Why did she have such a visceral reaction to Rust with that doctor? I had to hold my wolf back or she would have forced a shift. Not at all something I can allow, ever. And definitely not in front of humans. We're taught to control our wolves from the moment we're conscious of their presence within us. What the hell would trigger her?!

Mystified, I dab my face with a napkin from the food bag, then rise. I close my eyes and breathe deeply. Before I go to my office, I'll stop by the dispensary. The gods willing, the delayed medicines arrived. The risk proves too great without my serum.

CHAPTER 7

ust

"Oh, Rust! You're too funny!"

I smirk at the doctor as we enter the hospital's cafeteria. I have an hour before the start of my shift and decided to grab breakfast. She overhead me telling the ER nurses where to find me and asked to come with. Not one to deny a woman her desires, I welcomed her.

"I think I'll get a breakfast burrito. What about you?"

Undecided, I sniff the air for a scent that piques my tastebuds. Then stand gobsmacked.

Is it possible? Or a vestige from my carnal wet dream?

I spin in a slow circle with my head tilted back, nostrils flared.

Real or fake?

But damned if my wolf senses detect a faint trace of earth, ferns, and fir trees mix with a hint of vanilla carried on the cool ocean breeze. The unique scent of my fated mate on a she-wolf. Here. In the hospital's cafeteria???

Serum coats my canines as they extend to sharp fangs. The beat of my heart quickens and pulses in my ears. I stifle a groan as my cock grows down my inner thigh. Seed beads at the swollen tip. Fists form at my sides to restrain myself from throwing my head back and issuing a call to my fated mate.

Where is she?!

I scan the room. My eyes linger on each female. But none respond to the low rumble in my chest detectable by a she-wolf. She must have come and gone! I dash for the doors, ignoring the doctor's calls of my name. Carnal hunger for my fated mate supplants any need for mere food. My sole intent to find my fated mate. Now.

My wolf takes the lead to track her. The unique scent leads us to the elevators. As I growl in frustration, staring at the eight cars moving between twenty floors and the multitude of people, my wolf yips. I cock my head, then move towards the front doors of the hospital. Again, the scent picks up. Unfortunately, once outside, it dissipates in the wind. I stride back inside and pause, allowing my wolf to search for even the slightest whiff. Only the same trail back to the elevators.

I spend the next ten minutes popping my head into each elevator when it arrives on the ground floor. The humans stare at me, surprised by my unusual behavior. I ignore them.

A quick sniff finds nothing until the last car. The subtle combination of earth, ferns, and fir trees mixed with vanilla lingers in the air. I hurry inside and stand at the front. On each floor, I poke my head out for a quick whiff. Bingo!

Thirteen isn't an unlucky number!

I throw myself off the elevator and rush to the corridor. It branches in two directions. A few feet down, one proves she didn't pass this way. I retrace my steps and jog to the other wing. The scent increases. And my urge to claim my fated mate rises with it.

My vision tunnels. The rumble in my chest returns. Every female I pass gets an inconspicuous sniff. None in the hallway bears my fated mate's unique scent. I double back and enter the offices. The process repeats. I close the door of a supply closet, then turn to the last door at the end of the corridor.

As I near it, a familiar voice reaches my enhanced ears.

"Are you sure the medicines will arrive this afternoon? I mean, their delivery keeps getting delayed. Is there a way for you to confirm now?"

Natalie? In the dispensary asking about medicines again? An odd assortment of medicines typically not used by OB-GYNs?

The niggling I had the first time I saw her in the dispensary speaking to the pharmacist returns. What the hell would she need them for? Not a patient. And she's not ill.

It's highly inappropriate for doctors to use the hospital's dispensary for personal use. What is she up to? That reminds me of the quick recovery of her fractured arm and the glint in her eyes. None of it makes sense. Unless—

I'm so distracted by my thoughts, I don't notice her backing out the door until she bumps into me and yelps. Automatically, my hands reach out to steady her. The moment we connect, a bolt of electricity zings from my fingertips, up my arms, and straight to my pounding heart. A sharp intake of air carries the scent of my fated mate deep into my lungs. My cock twitches and leaks with seed. I growl.

She jerks her head around. Her wide onyx eyes meet my glowing hazel orbs. She gasps and tries to pull away. I tighten my grip and rumble in my chest. Her eyes flutter closed as she sags against me, mouth slack.

I ache to cover it with mine. Instead, I scoop her up and carry her to the empty supply closet. Her eyes pop open, and she protests. I silence her with a low growl. She shivers and glances away. Color suffuses her cheeks. Again, I fight the urge to kiss her and open the door, then flick on the overhead light. I continue to hold her close to my chest even after the door closes behind us.

"Natalie."

Her name comes out rough as my voice thickens with desire. She shivers and squirms. I bury my face in her hair. Then it hits me. Waist-long midnight hair with a snow-white widow's peak, just like the she-wolf in my wet dream. Except it wasn't a dream.

Fated mates often visit the other in dreams before they meet. The frequency and intensity increase the closer to them meeting in real life. A sort of bonding before the actual mate bonding ceremony occurs. In the dreams' vividness, the pair appear to be together in reality, not a dream—wet or otherwise. Sometimes they recognize one another. Often, they're not revealed, somehow shrouded or in wolf form, as with Natalie and me.

Dr. Natalie Moore. My fated mate. Fuck. Who knew? And how did I not detect her all this time?

"Put me down. Now!"

Her shriek rouses me from my musings.

"No!" I growl in response. "Tell me how you're an undetectable she-wolf. Now!"

"I have no idea what you're talking about! Let me go!"

"I will never let you go, Natalie. You are my fated mate. We belong together. You feel it as much as I do. I scent your arousal and hear the fast beat of your heart. The sooner you tell me what you've done, the sooner we can complete our mate bonding ceremony."

She freezes at my words.

I cock my head to the side to glimpse her face. But her hair covers it like a silky curtain. The bitter odor of fear rises in my nostrils. It overrides her arousal. What the fuck?!

"Natalie?"

Suddenly, she bucks her head. It crashes into my nose. Bone shatters as blood gushes. I stumble backwards and lose my hold on her. She slips to her feet and rounds on me. Onyx eyes flash.

"I reject you as my fated mate! I want no parts of you! Keep away from me!" She screams, then bolts for the door.

My hand flings out to grab her, but she wrenches to the side and evades my grasp. The door jerks open. She glares at me over her shoulder.

"I REJECT YOU, RUST INGOLF!"

She darts out the door. It slams shut. The sound of her feet pounding on the floor fades with the distance she puts between us. The thread that binds us snaps.

I throw my head back and howl in anguish, uncaring about the humans outside the door blood dripping down my front. My enhanced healing will repair my nose. But what about my broken heart?

NATALIE

I PANIC.

Pure adrenaline drives me to the max. I run like the hounds of Hell chase me. Too scared Rust will follow me, I skip waiting for an elevator and head for the staircase. I hurtle down three steps at a time until I land on the ground floor. A peek through the door's window confirms Rust isn't lurking around, waiting to drag me away and claim me as his fated mate.

Fated mate!

Just my rotten luck the moment my suppression serum wears off, I stumble across a wolf shifter who's my fated mate *and* a doctor in the same hospital as me. GAH!

I yank the door open and rush out of the hospital, heading for the safety of my car.

But it's Dr. McDreamy…

I ignore my inner voice and my wolf, who howls in anguish. Most of all, I ignore the agony in my heart. To reject a fated mate bond is akin to ripping your heart out with your bare hands. The bond severs. But the pain can last forever. Or drive the male into madness. My forehead drops to the steering wheel.

The ring of my mobile startles me. I scramble inside my crossbody bag to retrieve the device. For a second I think it's Rust. But he doesn't have my number. Thank the gods! I check the screen. The number for the OB-GYN department flashes.

I glance at the time. Dammit! I'm late for the staff meeting.

"H—Hello?"

"Natalie, the meeting started. Are you on your way?" Paloma Sabela asks.

My mind reels. If I go back inside the hospital, there's a chance Rust will track me to my office. As much as I don't want to face him, I have no choice but to go. And then what? How can I work in the same place as him and risk him claiming me despite my rejection?

I shudder as flashes of Sam and Amanda, then him

turning to me, run through my mind. No way can I allow myself to be forced into a mating. I have no other choice.

With a heavy heart, I tell Paloma Sabela I need to speak with the head of the department after the meeting. She's surprised but agrees to let him know. After we end the call, I gather my strength and return to the hospital. I slip into the conference room and take a seat in the rear.

"Dr. Moore, you wish to speak with me?"

"Yes, Dr. Wright. Unfortunately, I have an emergency that requires me to leave Miami. I—I—"

My voice cracks. I swallow past the lump in my throat as tears fill my eyes. I hang my head, defeated.

"Dr. Moore, I'm sorry to hear that and to see you so upset. I hope everything works out," he says, then pauses.

I lift my gaze as I dab my eyes. He offers me a fatherly smile.

"Might I suggest you take a leave of absence for a month? You had a terrible fall yet continued to treat patients, even saved a mother and her unborn baby. You're new to the team. However, we value your contributions in the short time you've been with the department. I'll make an exception for your leave should you wish to take time off instead of resigning. We would rather lose you for a few weeks than forever. Why don't you go home and give me your answer in the morning? I'll have another doctor cover for you today."

I sag in relief. Time off would give me time to make my serum and restart my injections. Perhaps with my wolf suppressed, the fated mate bond will disappear. Rust and I didn't know about it all this time. So, the chances of it disappearing again are pretty high.

But is it worth it? Do you really want to give up your heart of heart wish for a partner in life? A pack?

Once again, I ignore my inner voice.

I take a deep, cleansing breath.

"Thank you, Dr. Wright. You're more than generous with your offer. I thank you and accept."

"Excellent. Human Resources will reach out to you later today. Take care of yourself. If you're ready to return earlier than expected, call me."

He rises from the chair, and I follow. At the double doors, we part with a handshake. I express my gratitude again, and he smiles, wishing me the best.

Before I leave, I tell Paloma Sabela and Thandie. They wish me luck as we embrace. I smile to myself, happy to have new girlfriends. In my office, I take a few things I'll need during my leave, then head for the dispensary. I tell the pharmacist I'll send a messenger to pick up the medicines, and he agrees.

Tasks complete, I head for the parking lot. I glance around, half expecting Rust to leap from around a corner and drag me caveman style to his den. My wolf whines as she stares at me with dejected eyes. Sorry, I whisper.

As I pass the emergency room entrance, I spot dark ginger hair shining in the sunlight. My heart clenches. Unconsciously, I slow the car down.

Sensing my stare, Rust turns his head from the patient on the gurney. Our eyes meet.

Electricity sparks through me. I gasp and turn back to the road ahead. My eyes dart to the rearview mirror, drawn like a magnet to steel.

Rust stands in the middle of the road, eyes locked on mine.

CHAPTER 8

ust

"DAMN, bro! What the hell's gotten into you?"

"You look like shit!"

"I'd say look what the cat dragged in, except we're wolves…"

"Did somebody steal your favorite toy, or what?!"

Jagger, Viggo, Tag, and Dylan double over and high five one another. Their guffaws fill the air as they sit on the terrace of Jagger and Sage's bayfront mansion on Moon Island.

I can't summon the energy to respond to my best friends' inane comments, especially when they're spot on. It's been three days since Natalie rejected me as her fated mate. When our eyes connected and she continued to drive away from me, my heart broke anew. It's been pure torture. A needle hurts. But this pain… Ouch.

An ER nurse had to call me back to care for the incoming patient. Fortunately, it was a mild case of food poisoning, or I would have been beyond pissed with myself. For the rest of the day, I forced myself to focus. By the end of my shift, mental exhaustion set in. Not to mention the searing pain slicing my heart. The night proved no better. I tossed and turned with dreams of tracking Natalie only for her to dodge out of my reach.

The next two days, the pain from her rejection grew worse. Unable to concentrate, I took off two weeks starting today. The Director of Emergency Medicine was more than happy to approve my last-minute vacation request since I rarely take time off and bust my ass each shift. Plus, she took one glimpse of me and realized I needed a break.

Not wanting to stumble about my penthouse, I sent a text message to my boys to hang out. Hopefully, the distraction will ease the sorrow of finding then losing my fated mate after all these years. And stave off the madness I sense in my wolf. I rub my chest and drop onto a chaise lounge next to Viggo.

His ice blue eyes regard me. Those who don't know think we're brothers since he has long, red hair like mine. He wears his in a ponytail with the sides of his head buzzed. Pack tattoos adorn his scalp. A tribute to our Viking ancestors. Each of us—aside from Jagger—have paw prints on our pecs as symbolism for our bond as best friends for life.

He stretches his long legs in front of him and folds his bulging biceps across his chest.

"Speak up. What's going on?"

"I look like shit. I feel like shit. Not from the loss of a toy… But from my fated mate. She rejected me."

A hush descends. Hell, even the birds and insects stop chirping. A glance at each of my friends' faces reveals their stunned silent—eyes bug and mouths hang open. If I wasn't so torn up, I'd laugh at the sight of four Alpha males looking like cartoon characters.

"Your *fated mate*?" Tag asks, the first to recover from shock. Then his emerald green eyes narrow. "Where did you meet her?"

"Better yet, how the hell did you let her reject you? Damn!" Dylan chimes in.

Jagger sits forward, resting his elbows on his knees. He cocks his head to the side and studies me like his brother just did with the same ice blue eyes.

"Where is she?"

I shrug, then growl in frustration.

"Okay, start from the beginning," Jagger says.

I recall every detail from our first encounter in the emergency room to dinner after we teamed up to save the mother and her unborn baby to Natalie driving away. I even went to her apartment. She didn't answer, and I couldn't detect her scent. Since I couldn't sleep last night, I stood in the park across the street from her apartment and waited for hours, hoping to get a glimpse of her. Nothing. By the time I finish, their faces register pity and disbelief. Yeah, tell me about it.

Again, I rub the ache in my chest as I stare out over Biscayne Bay towards South Beach. The salty breeze from the Atlantic Ocean reminds me of Natalie's unique scent. I want to throw my head back and howl. My wolf whines.

Jagger opens his mouth to speak, then stands as a grin spreads across his face.

Dylan leaps to his feet.

"Hi, fellas! Sasha and I made too much popcorn for our movie night. We figured you might want some."

Sage followed by a heavily pregnant Sasha carries two giant bowls of buttered popcorn and a roll of paper towels. They sit them on the side tables. Sage wiggles from Jagger's arms and faces me.

"Oh, Rust! Your fated mate!" She exclaims as she walks towards me. She sits on the foot of Viggo's chaise lounge and holds her hands out to me. When I hesitate and glance at Jagger, who growls, she rolls her eyes. "He won't bite your head off if you hold my hands, Rust! You're in pain. Let me help you."

"Don't tempt me," he retorts.

She giggles, and her green eyes dazzle like emeralds. Shaking her head, she gestures with her hands palms up.

I place my palms on hers.

She yelps and yanks away. Jagger leaps at me, but she holds up her hands and laughs.

"Gotcha!"

Her laughter turns into a squeal when Jagger swoops her up and places her on his lap as he sits across from me. She settles, then turns to me.

"Okay, now, seriously. I can help you. But first you must promise not to force Natalie to mate with you, or I'll shrivel up your manhood without hesitation."

I don't even bother to ask how Sage knows about my fated mate or her name. As the High Witch and super powerful, there's nothing I would put past her wolf-enhanced magickal abilities. If she can help me with Natalie, I'm all in.

"I promise, Sage."

She studies my face, then nods.

"You have to be very careful with your fated mate. She's wounded"—Sage holds her hand up when I jump to my feet—"Not physically. In her heart. She's had a rough time in life. I won't divulge any more since it's her story to share with you. Again, not to be forced from her. Go to her now. She rented a little cottage in Big Pine Key for the month…"

Amazed by Sage's knowledge, I whip out my mobile and type in the address. Jagger offers the pack's Sikorsky S-92 Executive Helicopter to transport me to the key quickly. I call the pilot, and he confirms he'll meet me at the helipad in fifteen minutes.

Before I race from the deck, Sage invokes a spell to fix my sorry ass. Gone are the limp hair, three-day beard, and bags under my eyes. A glance at my reflection in the infinity pool proves she brought back my handsomeness—if I must say so myself. I thank her and rush off.

An hour later, I stand in front of a white picket gate separating the road from a path leading to the cottage set amongst palm trees and flowering shrubs. It's tranquil with beautiful scenery. At once, a sense of peace envelopes me. I close my eyes and inhale deeply. A trace of her unique scent carries over the floral bouquet. Thank the gods.

I lift the latch and step onto the path. After I secure the gate, I jog towards the front door. Her scent grows stronger with each step. My heartbeat increases, and my cock punches the zipper of my jeans. As I reach the door, a distressed cry from the rear of the cottage reaches my ears. Immediately, I'm on high alert. My protective instinct kicks in. I race around the corner, ready to defend my fated mate. My wolf's growl joins mine.

"Natalie!"

I shout her name when I see her sitting on the step of the back porch alone.

One hand squeezes her bare thigh while the other hand holds a syringe poised above her leg. Tears stream down her flushed cheeks. At my urgent cry, her head snaps up. Onyx eyes widen as her mouth opens on a gasp.

I dart forward faster than humanly possible and snatch the syringe from her hand. She jumps to her feet, reaching for the needle. I lift my arm to the sky.

"What the fuck are you doing?! What drug is this?"

She flinches at my harsh tone.

I don't give a fuck! I will not allow her to harm herself. It's hard to cope when separated from a fated mate. But it's not enough to turn to drugs. If that were the case, then

Jagger would have thrown my ass in rehab instead of me coming here. I scowl as I tower over her.

"Rust, it's not what you think. Please, just give it back."

"Not until you tell me what's in the syringe."

She swipes her hand over her face and walks up the porch steps. At the back door, she glances over her shoulder.

"Come inside. I don't want to talk out here."

I sniff the air. No deceit, only a profound sadness surrounds her. My mind recalls Sage's words about Natalie's wounded heart. Time to learn more about my fated mate.

NATALIE

RUST FOLLOWS me into the house. I shut the door behind him and gesture towards the living room. I run my suddenly sweaty palms on the front of my strapless romper. When I glance up, Rust has a glint in his hazel eyes. His wolf is near the surface. I shiver and hurry to the kitchen for some bottles of water. When I return, he still has a wolfish expression on his handsome face. My wolf preens happy to be near our fated mate.

And fated mate, he is.

I couldn't bear to remain in Miami, knowing Rust was so close to my apartment. Its proximity to the hospital proved inconvenient when trying to avoid him. I didn't want to leave the state. A search on the Internet brought up the Florida Keys with Big Pine Key being the most mellow. Perfect for me to be alone and think about what I want to do with my life. More importantly if I wanted Rust in it. I booked the cottage for the rest of my leave.

When the medicines arrived from the hospital dispensary, I made my suppression serum and packed two vials and syringes. My wolf was back fully. All my senses returned. Plus, the inherent desire to belong to a pack and to have a mate.

I wrestled with the pros and cons for the last three days. Never alone again. Potential for love. No fear of Sam finding me and forcing me back to Washington since Rust's pack's Alpha wouldn't allow it to happen. But then I'd have to give up my career. Bow down to a male. Be bred for pups. Gah!

The days of debate are bad. But the nights filled with erotic dreams starring Dr. McDreamy keep me in a heightened state of arousal. My full breasts are heavy tipped with sensitive nipples. Constant pulses of my pussy walls clenching on air—or on my fingers. Dreams so real I wake sweaty and dripping. Double Gah!

Many times, I wonder if Rust aches for me as I do for him. Or if he found solace in the arms of that doctor or any of the nurses who fawn all over him. Worse yet, between their welcoming thighs. Talk about triple gah!

Then when I build the courage to put an end to the debate and my misery, Rust appears out of thin air! So, intent on my task, I didn't detect his presence. I nearly had a coronary.

Now, I stare at him and wonder. Was I about to make a terrible mistake suppressing my wolf again? He came for me. That counts as something. But how did he find me? I'll ask after I tell him about the serum and what forced me to suppress my wolf. And more importantly, drive me away from him—my fated mate.

"Here's a water," I say as I sit on the love seat. I shake my head at how apropos the name.

"Thank you," Rust says as he sits beside me.

His nearness engulfs me in his citrusy, musky, and spicy scent. He's pure masculinity as his long, muscular legs spread. His thigh presses against mine, and I have to bite back a wanton moan. It's bad enough my nipples pucker beneath the terrycloth of my romper. Their outline apparent since I don't wear a bra.

He cocks his head and sniffs. A feral growl rumbles in his chest as he pins me with a stare full of lust and possessiveness.

My pussy spasms.

"Natalie…"

I nearly cum from the silken baritone growl of my name dripping from his lush mouth. My eyelids droop as I breathe past my parted lips. Heat warms my cheeks and seeps into my pussy. I scent my own arousal. It turns me on more.

A large hand wraps around the back of my neck and pulls me forward. My wide eyes jump to Rust's flashing hazel ones. His mouth a hair's breadth away from mine. He sucks in my pants, then crashes his mouth on mine.

The world tilts.

White stars shoot behind my closed eyelids.

Sound ceases except for his growls and my moans.

All thoughts fly from my head.

My fingers bunch around the front of his t-shirt as I cling to him to keep from spinning into orbit.

His tongue thrusts inside of my mouth. It swirls around to taste every corner, then laps my tongue. Teeth nip my swollen lips. He tilts my head by his grip on my neck to better the angle for him to devour me whole.

The all-encompassing kiss goes on for what seems to be eternity. My lungs burn for air. I turn my head as best I can to catch my breath. Rust growls and trails open-mouthed kisses from the corner of my slack mouth, across my jaw, and down the column of my throat. When his canines graze the juncture of my neck and shoulder, I yelp.

Reality sets in, and I realize I'm somehow straddling his thighs perched above his hard, massive cock. It rocks up against my slippery pussy lips. Only thin scraps of cotton and his jeans separate us from mating.

My palms slam against his firm chest. It's like hitting a brick wall. He's oblivious to my sudden distress... Hot moisture drips onto my skin. His mouth opens wide.

"MINE!"

Oh, gods, no!

"Rust! Stop!"

ust

"RUST! STOP!"

Natalie's scream freezes me. Her tiny fists pound my chest as she jerks away from me. She tumbles from my lap to land on her ass. Without missing a beat, she crab walks backwards until she bumps into the opposite wall. Her eyes full of fright watch me warily.

Still caught in a lust-filled possessive haze, I rise and stride towards her with my hand outstretched.

"NO! GRRRR…"

Her onyx eyes flash. The grinding sounds of bones reshaping and muscles lengthening fill the room. Her oval face morphs into a snout full of sharp teeth evident behind her curled lip as she snarls. As she moves to her hands and feet, her eyes never leave mine. Amidst a crackling, a flash, and ripping cloth, her wolf appears with midnight fur and a white streak like her widow's peak. The she-wolf of my dreams.

Except this time, her hackles rise, tail flicks back and forth, and she growls menacingly. No affectionate playfulness and damn sure no carnal desire apparent. She's prepared to attack.

Although she's larger than a regular wolf, she's no match for me, even in my human form. Especially when the need to mark, claim, and mate her ramp up my wolf and me.

But I set aside our bonding since something spooked her. I recall Sage's words and Natalie's initial plan to talk. With an inward groan, I rein in my wolf and lower my hand.

"Natalie, you are my fated mate—"

She growls and leaps with her fangs exposed and her claws extended. Her movement is clumsy, as though she and her wolf don't sync. Regardless, she's still capable of damage.

Instinct takes over. I dodge to the side. She flies past me and lands on the love seat, then whips around with a growl prepared to pounce. Oh. Hell. No.

"SHIFT!" I roar, instilling my Alpha command over my fated mate.

Already in the air, she crumples to the floor. Her wolf recedes immediately. She curls into a protective fetal position, covering her naked body as she trembles. Muffled sobs reach my ears.

My heart clenches. I drop to my knees and pull her onto my lap. My arms band about her body, pressing her close to my rumbling chest. She protests weakly. But eases against me as the soothing sound calms her. I murmur words of love against the delicate shell of her ear.

"Natalie, my heart, I did not mean to frighten you. Tell me what I did that spooked you," I say after her sobs slow to hiccups.

She squirms on my lap. Now it's my cock screaming for release.

I throw my head back and groan, "Babe, keep still, or I'll blow inside my jeans."

Her movements stop abruptly. The bitter scent of fear mixes with her unique scent.

Fuck!

Why does she get upset about sex? Did a male force himself on her? If someone did, I'll rip his fucking head off. In fact, both big and small! The thought makes me growl.

"Rust, just let me go."

I hold her chin between my thumb and forefinger as I turn her head to align our eyes.

"What did I tell you before?"

Her eyes dart away. But I wiggle her chin, and she glances back at me.

"I will never let you go, Natalie. You are my fated mate. We belong together. You feel it as much as I do. Remember?"

She nods. I cock an eyebrow.

The tip of her little pink tongue flicks out and sucks her lower lip inside her mouth. Her teeth dimple in the flesh.

My cock jumps in my jeans.

"Yes, *Rust*."

Yeah, Fuck. Me.

"But I need to put on some clothes before we talk."

"You might as well get used to being naked, especially on my lap, Little Girl. When we are alone, I want you bare to me. I want to feast upon you with my eyes, mouth, fingers, and cock at all times. You are too beautiful to cover in unnecessary clothes that hamper my access. Do you understand?"

She bristles. Her wolf flashes in her eyes, ready to spring forth yet again. She slaps at my arms around her waist.

"You see! That's what's wrong with you male wolves! It's always about you and your needs. The gods forbid if a she-wolf has a thought of her own or her desires differ! I didn't let Sam force me to mate, and I won't let you either! No matter how much I ache for you!"

Her eyes widen in surprise at her last words. But mine narrow at the former.

"Who the *fuck* is Sam?!"

She startles at my possessive roar. Then regains her feistiness. She folds her arms across her full tits. The heart-shaped birthmark on the inner curve of her left breast catches my eye. I doubt she realizes she's made them more pronounce since she glares at me and doesn't hide.

"Do *not* yell at me!"

Okay, this is going nowhere. Reel it in, Rust. I suck in a breath as I close my eyes, then exhale as they reopen, focused on my angry fated mate. Crimson heats her cheeks. I do my best to ignore the tantalizing rise and fall of her heaving chest. Instead, I grip her waist and squeeze. She yelps and blinks. Now that I have her attention...

"Natalie, I know we have a lot to learn about one another. So, you wouldn't know I am an Alpha dominant. My kink is sexual control of my submissive partner to bring her ecstasy unlike ever experienced. I have no desire to control you outside of sex. Nor force you into anything you do not want. Even accepting my claiming bite to bond with me forever. I'll likely go mad. But rather my biggest fear than to hurt you. I do not know *Sam*. But I can assure you we are nothing alike. Do you understand?"

She studies my face for a moment and sniffs the air to detect any guile. Finding none, she relaxes.

"Yes, Rust, I understand. And you're right. From what I've seen and heard, you are an honorable male wolf who cares more for others than for himself. You're the complete opposite of Sam. That's why we need to talk. I want to explain things to you."

She pauses with an arched eyebrow and tugs on my t-shirt.

"As much as being your naked plaything appeals to me, I would rather have this conversation clothed."

I grin at her admission. She purses her lips.

As I grab the back of my t-shirt, I press my mouth to

hers, then nip the plump bottom lip. She moans as I pull it before I yank my t-shirt over my head.

Through hooded eyes, she ogles my chiseled pecs and eight-pack abs. Her gaze follows the red feathery trail until it dips below the waistband of my low-slung jeans. Mesmerized, she drags a fingernail along the hair. Her eyes widen when my cock twitches in my jeans. And fuck if her sweet arousal punches the air between us.

I inhale deeply and lick my lips with a low growl. She blushes prettily and lifts her arms to pull my t-shirt on. My mouth salivates as her juicy tits jounce. The beaded rosy tips beg for me to suckle them. Hard. They disappear beneath the soft cotton, but their outline winks at me.

"Eyes up here, mister," she says as she lifts my chin up with her index finger.

I dip my head in deference, then raise it with a scowl when she slips from my lap to sit on the floor beside me. I catch her thighs and pull her back. She shakes her head. Silky midnight strands sway around her face and down her back. She runs a hand through the white streak and blows a breath.

"That anaconda you're packing is too much of a distraction. I need some space to think straight."

I chuckle and acquiesce. But I keep her legs over my lap. She rolls her eyes and stays put. Then she takes a deep breath.

"My name is Natalie Glenns, youngest daughter of deceased Alpha Conchar Glenns and deceased Luna Eilín Glenns, younger sister to deceased Amanda Dunne, née

Glenns, and aunt to deceased pup Aidan Dunne of the Olympia Wolves Pack in Washington State."

My fated mate's eyes fill with tears and her voice stutters as she speaks of her family. She swipes the tears with her fingers and continues. I bring her fingers to my mouth and kiss each one, licking the tears into my mouth. She swallows and smiles softly as her fingertips stroke my lips.

"My parents died from an unexpected affliction two years before my sister and her stillborn pup died in childbirth. Many of our members died with my parents, as did many she-wolves who were forced to breed to increase our losses. Unfortunately, Sam Dunne fought for and won the role of Alpha after my father passed away. He forced my sister to marry him, as she was the eldest daughter of the former Alpha, and Sam wanted to benefit from the prestige of my family's legacy. The moment she took her last breath with Aidan in her arms, Sam turned to me and told me I would replace my sister as his mate. After I buried my sister and nephew beside my parents, I left my former pack that night."

Her lower lip wobbles as more tears flow. I lift her onto my lap, away from my now flaccid cock. She rests her head against my rumbling chest. The vibrations lull her. With fingers twined in mine, she continues to tell me about her desire to help pregnant women and their unborn babies. The long hours of studying at college and medical school to finish early and with honors, then performing well during her residency. Her goal to make her applications appealing to the best OB-GYN departments in the nation.

And how she chose Miami since it's furthest from her former pack.

I tell her how I admire her drive and determination. She smiles softly but puts a finger to my lips and shakes her head.

"I had no desire to be amongst wolf shifters and no interest in a mate or pups. To avoid detection, I created a serum to suppress my wolf"—I balk, and she shakes her head rapidly—"Let me finish, Rust. The medicines from the hospital dispensary are meant to replace my supply I dropped the night I fell from the stepladder and landed in the ER. With you."

She pauses to stare at me intensely. Sharp onyx eyes pierce my soul as she searches for any sign of judgment. I keep my expression open. She nods and goes on to explain the process and the return of her wolf.

My mind reels with her incredible discovery. Never have I heard of any shifter being able to suppress its animal half. Nothing in the Viking ancient texts I studied to learn their healing knowledge relayed anything of the sort.

Now, I understand how she went undetected by my wolf and by me. Plus, she couldn't scent me as a wolf shifter. Amazing but dangerous.

"Natalie, I doubt it, but I have to ask. Have you shared your serum with anyone?"

"Absolutely not. If it were to get in the wrong hands..." She lets her words trail off as we both know the impact the serum could have on shifters and humans. And with her being the only one with the knowledge, she's vulnerable.

I growl and hug her closer to me. She nuzzles against my neck, placing her palm over my heart. Her touch soothes me, and I bury my face in her silky hair.

"Now, do you understand my trust issues and negative reaction to you proclaiming us fated mates?" She asks softly.

I press a kiss to the crown of her head.

"Who can blame you? I get it."

"And I can never let Sam find me. I don't know what he'd do. But the thought of leaving the other she-wolves under his and his cronies' thumbs sickens me. I just wish I knew how to save them."

I sit back to stare directly into her eyes. Mine glow with my wolf who snarls and paces.

"Natalie Glenns Moore soon to be Ingolf, you are my fated mate. I will protect you and our pups with my life. Any threat to you I will destroy. Fear no one. Do you understand?"

Without hesitation, she responds, "Yes, Rust."

"Good, girl. And you needn't worry about the she-wolves. We will call my pack's Alpha—about that fucker Sam's wrongdoings. I'm sure the Alpha of the Los Angeles Wolves Pack will not appreciate one of the packs within his territory harming she-wolves. We treasure our females. Those with mates—fated or not—and unmated deserve the pack's respect, love, and care."

"Rust, are you sure? Do you think they'll really help?" My fated mate asks eyes full of hope.

I nod and reposition her on my lap to reach into my pocket for my mobile. I pull up the FaceTime app.

"We'll call him right now. I don't want you to worry another minute."

She squeezes my arm as a brilliant smile spreads across her face.

"Thank you!"

Our gazes shift to the mobile screen. It connects with Jagger's on video.

"Rust. What's happening?"

"Alpha—"

"Oh, so, this call must be pretty damn serious for you to call me Alpha instead of Jagger—"

"Rust! You didn't upset her, did you? I warned you. Don't think I can't get to you from here!" Sage says as she leans over Jagger's shoulder to glare at me through the screen.

Fuck if my cock and balls don't shrivel just at the thought of Sage making good on her threat. I shake my head vigorously.

"No, Luna. I didn't upset Natalie. In fact, she's right here on my lap," I respond, adjusting the mobile's angle to include her face.

"Thank the Fates!" Sage declares.

Jagger pulls her onto his lap, and she leans against him with her emerald green eyes focused on Natalie to confirm she's fine.

"But we do have a major problem, one that involves the Los Angeles Wolves Pack."

Jagger sits up and narrows his eyes as they flash cobalt with his wolf near the surface. As Natalie recounts her story, his anger rises. At the end, he growls and assures Natalie the Los Angeles Alpha will rectify the situation immediately. She expresses her gratitude. He nods.

"Natalie, as Rust's fated mate, my Luna and I welcome you to the Miami Wolves Pack. Not only will your fated mate protect you, so will every male in our pack. I will finish anyone who dares to threaten you or to enter my territory to challenge Rust for you. More than likely, Magnus will punish the so-called alpha of your former pack, along with his followers severely. But do not worry about retribution."

"You will meet Sasha, another new member of our pack and the fated mate of Dylan—one of Jagger and Rust's best friends. It's her story to tell. But I guarantee it will resonate with you, Natalie," Sage adds.

Jagger nods, then asks, "Should we expect you back in a week after your seclusion? We can plan for a pack run in the Everglades to welcome Natalie officially."

"Yes! And your mate bonding ceremony!" Sage says as she bounces on Jagger's lap, clapping her hands. "I loved Jagger's and mine! So romantic!"

My fated mate stiffens on my lap and turns her head from the mobile screen. Tension fills the air. She tries to rise, but I tighten my arm around her waist. I cock my head and stare at her profile. She won't meet my gaze.

Jagger and Sage sit in silence.

"Natalie?" I ask.

She mumbles a response, and I pray to the gods my enhanced wolf hearing mistook her words.

"Natalie?"

She faces me and repeats words that sear my soul.

"I did not agree to mate you, Rust."

CHAPTER 10

atalie

IF A FACE COULD COLLAPSE, Rust's would crumble to dust like a skyscraper hit by a dozen wrecking balls. His skin pales as his eyebrows dip over dimmed hazel eyes. The corners of his mouth droop. A gust of air puffs from between his parted lips. They move to form words, then close. He squeezes his eyes shut and shakes his head. When he opens them and stares at me, they're full of anguish.

My heart clenches.

"Uh, we'll let you go, Rust."

"And remember what I said about your manhood."

His Alpha and Luna's voices sound from afar as I stare back into Rust's eyes. He winces at Sage's words. I find them odd, but don't dare to ask their meaning while he's shocked by my response.

I'm a bit taken aback too. My reaction to his unexpected appearance and to our heated kisses proves I'm attracted to Rust. Hell, if I'm perfectly honest, my body burns for him. My wolf rolled over and bared her vulnerable underbelly and throat to him. Well, after she came out to protect me when he tried to issue his claiming bite.

And that's it. I don't know if I want to be claimed. My views on being mated have changed since Rust. But I'm not sure I want to make that commitment. At least not right away.

He even admitted we don't know one another.

How can I just bow down and take his bite without a second thought? My former pack consisted of selected mates through alliances or choice before Sam forced she-wolves to mate. I've never witnessed a *fated* mate pair.

They're like a fairy tale where the two spy the other across a moonlit meadow and sparks fly between them. A sparkly tether appears at each one's heart and draws the pair together. Their hearts beat as one pulsing across the special bond. They embrace. The she-wolf tilts her head to the side, exposing her neck. The male wraps his arms around her, tips her backwards, and lowers his mouth to her neck. He bites, and she moans. They complete their bond by coupling as fireworks explode to twinkle with the stars above, and they live happily ever after. The End.

As I stare back at Rust, I wonder if we could actually be fated mates. Sure, he insists it's true, and I feel some sort of way about him. But forever is a long time. What if I give in now because he makes all these promises and later, he changes his mind? I'll end up stuck with him. Forever. Gah!

I glance away and attempt to rise from his lap. His arms tighten around me. When I face him, gone is anguish. Instead, gold flecks in his hazel eyes flash with his wolf. I blink at their fierceness and gasp at the pulse in my pussy.

"Already you forget I will never let you go, Natalie. Despite your hesitation, we belong together, fated mate. However, I won't beg you nor force you to accept my claiming bite. But you will tell me why you reject me. Again."

I lower my eyes as I nibble on my lower lip. How do I tell him what I want without contradicting myself? My lip pops from between my teeth as I yelp.

"Stop thinking so hard and answer with your heart, fated mate," Rust says as he squeezes my hip bones. He tightens his grip as I wiggle away. "Enough. Now, answer me."

As when he commanded I shift back from my wolf, words tumble from my mouth. I tell him my concerns about commitment, never witnessing fated mates, moving too fast, his promises being broken, all of it in one continuous stream. I let go and share it all. By the end, my mind clears. A sense of relief washes over me. I know what I want.

"Rust, I need time to get to know you and you me. It's not easy for me to forget wounds from my past and jump into a relationship forever. Your Alpha mentioned a week. Did you take time off from the hospital?"

"Yes, two weeks, actually, and I will extend it to four since you have the cottage for that amount of time. Let's stay here with no outside interference, no patients, no pack. Just you and me. I guarantee *you* will beg *me* to claim you before the end."

Somehow, I don't doubt it. But I don't admit it to him. Instead, I ask for what I've wanted from the moment I awoke drenched in sweat with a throbbing, soaked pussy.

"Fuck me, Rust."

~

Rust

"*Fuck me, Rust.*"

My eyes bug out as my jaw hits to the floor. My fated mate giggles and places the tip of her index finger beneath my chin to close my mouth. She leans over and seals it with her lips. Her tongue licks around its edges, then along its seam.

On a groan, I cup her ass and pull her onto my lap. Her thighs straddle my hips. I grip the back of her neck to position her head at an angle for me to dominate the kiss. She needs to know from the start I'm in control. My Alpha Dom and my wolf growl in agreement.

I swallow each of her breathy moans as my tongue

probes the wet warmth of her mouth. It thrusts inside and laps at her tongue. I groan when her hips undulate with the erotic rhythm I set. Her hot pussy lips rub against my burgeoning cock.

I guess she wears a thong since her juices soak my jeans. My fingers slip beneath my t-shirt to caress her waist and find the strips of cotton. I follow their trail to the patch of fabric covering her mons. A groan slips into her mouth when I feel her smooth and bare mons.

"Fuuuck, baby."

My teeth nip her lower lip as my thumb seeks her clit hidden by its hood. Slow circles make it swell. She gasps against my demanding mouth. Her pussy grinds down. I slide my middle finger past her slippery folds. She's so tight, my knuckle barely gets past. I jiggle it around to caress the sensitive spot on her front wall.

"Oh, *gods*!"

"Not the gods, baby. You're fated mate," I murmur against her panting mouth as I increase the strokes on her G-spot and engorged clit. Her cunt clenches and sucks my finger deeper as she screams.

My fangs descend, and the claiming serum drips along their length. I have to jerk my mouth away from hers to keep it from her neck. My vow to not force her and Sage's words prevent me from sinking my canines into my fated mate's flesh.

I cup her ass and flip us over, then settle between her trembling thighs. With a growl, I lower my mouth to drink from her gushing pussy. She bucks when the flat of my tongue strokes from clit to puckered hole. I growl and lay the flat of my palm against her lower belly and grip her ass with the other hand. Locked in place, she can only moan as I plunder her pussy with my tongue and teeth. My fingers spread her pussy lips wide. I flick my tongue up and down over her clit as I watch her.

After two more orgasms, her fingers tug at my hair.

"R—R—Rust… p—please…" She cries.

I lift my gaze up the length of her body. Our eyes connect.

"Tell me what you need, fated mate."

Bowing from the floor, her eyes close as she shudders. Another orgasm rips through her cunt, gripping my fingers like a vise. I wrap my tongue around her clit and suck. Hard. She wails. I swear she rips strands of my hair from the scalp. Ignoring the erotic pain, I swallow her juices in gulps. My eyes drag to her face. Her eyes remain closed. I spank her pussy lips, and her eyes pop open. The unfocused onyx orbs stare in my direction.

"Tell me!" I command. "Tell me what you need, my fated mate."

"YOU! I want you!"

My nostrils flare. I wipe my mouth of her juices on her inner thigh, then prowl up her body. My feral gaze never waivers as I keep hers pinned. One fist presses into the floor beside her head while the other hand tugs at the zipper of my jeans. My turgid cock springs free. I fist the base and drag my length along her sopping seam.

Her eyes roll to the back of her head. I growl, and she brings her lust-filled gaze back to mine.

"FUUUCK! Oh, Rust, Rust… Please fuck me!"

It's all the invitation I need. My tip lines up with her pussy. I bring my gaze to hers, wanting to see her reaction the first time I make her mine. Eyes wide and lip caught between her teeth, she watches me. My hands grip her hips and tilt her pelvis. I snap my hips forward and impale her on my cock in one swift thrust, buried balls deep in her tight little pussy.

She screams. Fingernails dig into the corded muscles of my forearms. Whether she pushes or pulls, I do not know. My instinct to take my fated mate and make her mine rides me hard. I growl her name with each pistoning stroke.

In return, her pussy walls clamp around my dick. It's a battle to withdraw as it sucks me in deeper. I groan with the effort. She syncs to my rhythm and rocks her hips to meet each of my savage thrusts. Her cries of passion match my possessive grunts and growls. It's a carnal symphony enhanced by the mingled musky scent of our fucking.

Before I give in to my own pleasure, I want another orgasm from my fated mate. One where she screams my name. I lick my fingers and reach between us. Thumb and forefinger roll, then pinch her clit as I nip the beaded tips of her tits through my t-shirt.

Her cry of my name while her cunt spasms around my cock makes my heavy balls fill with seed. The controlled thrusts give way to frantic hammering as I chase my release.

A tingle at the base of my spine increases to a lightning bolt. It zips along my nerve endings as it travels to my balls and along my cock. With a ferocious roar, I drive into her soaked pussy one last time. Plunged to my root, I growl as my cock grows impossibly bigger and the base of it expands.

She hisses as my knot wedges behind her pelvis to lock her to me. Her claws drag along my flanks as she howls from the stretch and burn. She thrashes beneath me, then keens when her pussy constricts for another orgasm.

It triggers my release. A long and low groan pours from my mouth as copious amounts of hot seed shoot from my cock to coat my fated mate's welcoming womb. Feral dominance and desire urge me to spill every last drop of my seed inside of her. I want her belly round with my pup.

"MINE! You. Are. Mine. Natalie. Only. Mine."

I punctuate each word with a determined thrust. Once again, I have to stop myself from issuing my claiming bite on my fated mate. It's a struggle as I force my fangs to retract while reining in my determined wolf. I close my eyes and howl.

She joins in as she clings to me.

Fully spent, I collapse on top of her. She holds me close and presses her lips to mine. Tears shine in her onyx eyes. I brush my lips against the lids and sigh. Our pants mix as I stare at my beautiful fated mate.

With enough air in my lungs, I wrap my arms around her and roll onto my back. Her smaller frame rests atop my much larger body. Her cheek over to my heart, I rumble to soothe her as I caress her back. She sighs and reaches up to twine her fingers in my hair. My knot will keep us connected for some time, so I allow my eyes to drift shut, content my fated mate rests in my arms. And this is no dream.

NATALIE

"BABY, why didn't you tell me? I thought you were tight. But I didn't realize—"

I place a finger over Rust's lips and shake my head.

"Please, don't. It was my choice. I didn't want you to treat me any differently than you did. I wanted all of you. Not a watered-down version because I was a virgin. Besides, no matter how gentle you may have been, that anaconda would still have split me in two!"

He chuckles and nips my finger.

"Split you in two, did I? How about we soak in the tub? The warm water will soothe your sore little pussy. And as much as it strokes my ego to know I'm the only male you'll ever know, I can rinse your virginal blood from my cock."

Naturally, my eyes go to his cock. It's so large I can't believe it even fits inside of me. And it's still erect! Suddenly shy, my cheeks heat. I can only nod as I avert my eyes from his crotch.

"Look at me, Natalie," he says in his commanding tone. When my eyes meet his, he directs his gaze to his cock. I flush deeper and nibble my lower lip. "Not my face, my cock. That's better. You have no reason to be shy with me or to avoid looking at my body. And damn sure not with me looking at yours. You said you want us to know each other. Well…"

He's got me there. I smile and stand. With a smirk, he tucks the anaconda away. I extend my hand to him. He takes it and rises. I squeal when he scoops me up, bridal style.

"Which way to the bathroom, fated mate? It's time I take care of you."

I tell him, and he strides out of the living room.

As we soak, I lean my back against his front. Rust makes good on his word. I all but melt as he washes and conditions my hair. His strong fingers knead my scalp, and I moan. It gets even better when he adds lavender-scented bath gel to a sponge and washes every inch of my body. But once again, I balk when he reaches between my thighs to clean my nether bits. He cocks an eyebrow.

"Last warning, Little Girl. Do not shy away from me— eyes or touch. Next time, I will take you across my knees and spank you soundly. Do you understand?"

My mouth gapes as my eyes skitter across his face. A serious glint in his hazel orbs lets me know he's not joking. No one spanked me as a child and certainly not as an adult. But instead of being outraged, my nipples pebble as heat pools in my lower belly. My pussy clenches. I bite back a moan as my thighs press together. The water sloshes over the sides of the clawfoot bathtub.

"Ah, ah, ah, Naughty Girl. Only I give you pleasure. You do not seek your own unless I give you permission. Now answer my question."

His reprimand adds fuel to the furnace raging in my pussy. He must sense my desire and maneuvers me to my knees with my fingers wrapped around the rim of the bathtub. He positions himself behind me and pulls my hips back. The head of his cock brushes along my wet slit. It nudges at my entrance, then sinks in slowly.

I moan wantonly as every vein, every ridge, and every inch of his long, thick cock strokes my inner walls. They suck him in greedily. At this angle, he goes deeper than before. I cry out. He fists my freshly cleaned hair and pulls my head back. My body bows and my pelvis tilts. He pushes in deeper as his mouth swallows my mewl.

Fully seated, groin to ass, his heavy balls slap my clit. I whimper in his mouth. He nips my lips. Long, even strokes of his cock have me white knuckling the edge of the bathtub. Again and again, he breaches my pussy with his slow drags.

I shudder as the first tingles of my orgasm surface. Wanting it to break, I push back against Rust.

He growls and withdraws. I cry out from the sudden loss and glance over my shoulder, only for his sizable palm to press between my shoulder blades. It holds me in place firmly. My mouth opens to protest.

THWACK. THWACK. THWACK. THWACK.

Instead of words, a startled yelp pops out of my mouth as his other palm spanks each of my ass cheeks in succession. Left. Right, Right. Left. It doesn't land on the same spot. But the sting blooms across my entire ass.

He wedges his thigh between my mine to widen my knees. The palm on my back presses down.

I should have known it wouldn't be good.

I nearly jump out of my skin when three of his fingers smack my swollen pussy lips. The squelching from my juices and the water minimizes the thwacking sound. But it does nothing for the erotic bite of pain. I bleat and try to move away. He holds me firm and leans over my back. Lips pressed to my ear, he speaks.

"For a smart little girl, you don't listen very well, Little Girl. Now, let's try this again."

He slides the palm on my back around the front of my throat. His other arm bands around my waist. In one punishing thrust, his cock fills my tight little pussy.

My mouth opens in a silent wail.

He withdraws, then slams back in. Over and over.

"Uh. Uh. Uh. Uh."

The only sound I can form as he sets a brutal pace. I love it.

My pussy flutters all along his thick length, trying to capture him for longer than a second. The rougher he mounts me, the more my arousal amps up and drips down my inner thighs. As much as I want to match his strokes, I can't. His hold allows no movement other than my breasts bouncing and my ass jiggling with each impact from his groin. I give in and sag against his hands.

"There's my good Little Girl. You please me. Now, cum for me."

I preen along with my wolf at his praise. Then fall under his erotic thrall as he continues to fuck me. My body responds to his command. The orgasm he abruptly stopped races forward not with tingles. An inferno rages through me. My eyes roll back, my pussy constricts, and my toes curl. All. At. Once.

"*OH, GODS!*"

Rust chuckles wickedly.

"Not the gods, Little Girl. YOUR. FATED. MATE!"

He explodes within me with a roar and triggers a mind-blowing orgasm.

As I pass out from the intensity of it all, my last thought makes me moan.

This is going to be the most excruciatingly tempting four weeks of my life. If Rust keeps this erotic torture up, I may just beg for his claiming bite. Gods help me…

CHAPTER 11

ust

"GOOD MORNING, sleepyhead. Did you get enough rest?"

I snicker and kiss my fated mate on the crown of her head

She's adorable, all tousled, barefoot, and dressed in one of my new t-shirts. It reaches the middle of her toned thighs. The much larger size does little to hide the swells of her tits topped with pebbled nipples. As she turns to sit at the kitchen table, I swat her ass and grin as it jiggles. She yelps and covers it with her hands as she scowls at me over her shoulder.

"I would if you didn't fuck me every five seconds, every single day and night," she responds with an arched eyebrow.

Yeah. I may not have issued my claiming bite to her. However, I initiated a seclusion where I kept her in bed, fucking her often for the last seven days. My goal? Get her hooked on my fine skills and used to begging me—to let her cum, that is. Soon she'll beg for me to make her mine completely. And I cook for her, bathe her, and treat her like a queen. I'm pulling out all stops to secure my fated mate.

Even so, she can be a naughty girl. Not that I mind her spunk. Keeps things spicy. I just don't let her know how much it turns me on.

I cock my eyebrow and let my eyes rove over her body. She begins to flush, but her nipples poke against the soft cotton. The scent of her arousal wafts through the air.

"You do not have that tone of voice when I pound your greedy little pussy, Little Girl. In fact, you barely speak at all. Only moans, whimpers, and howls of carnal pleasure pour from that sassy mouth of yours."

Crimson floods her cheeks as she lowers her gaze.

"Exactly. Now, let's have some breakfast. I planned a fun excursion for us."

She lifts her head. Onyx eyes sparkle in the sunlight from the kitchen windows. She claps her hands and shimmies on the wooden chair.

"Ooh! Where are we going?"

"It's a surprise. So, eat up, and we'll get going," I respond with a smirk as I slide an omelet onto her plate. Then chuckle when she digs in with gusto. "Slow down, babe. No need to rush."

When I turn back to the stove, she slaps my bare ass. I growl.

"Nice apron."

I glance down at the words written on the front and frown at her.

"It reads, *Kiss the Chef*, not Slap the Chef."

She giggles.

"Oops, my bad, *Chef*. Shall I make it better for you?" Her eyes sparkle with mischief.

Yup, my naughty fated mate. And I'd have her no different.

An hour later, the Uber pulls up to the marina. I take Natalie's hand and help her from the car. She glances around at the boats along the dock as we walk towards the end.

"We're getting on a boat?"

"Surprise! We're spending the week on our pack's boat."

Well, technically, it's Jagger's megayacht *Moonbeam*. He designed it with our pack in mind, wanting to provide the members with a luxurious water respite. The 465-foot silver megayacht has five decks tiered from the back with a long front to accommodate a helipad. Twenty cabins sleep up to thirty-six guests. For entertainment, it features a beach club with a garage for water sports toys, fitness center, spa and sauna, swimming pool and hot tub, media room, bowling alley, and a game room. Multiple living spaces include salons, wet bars, dining rooms, library, and an office with a conference room he can conduct business.

I called him to reserve it for my fated mate and me. It'll

give us the perfect way to explore the rest of the Florida Keys. I want her to experience all the pack and her new home has to offer. She wants to get the know me. Well, no better way than aboard the beauty.

Jagger was more than happy to arrange our excursion. So happy with his fated mate, he wants the rest of his best friends to have the same joy. Dylan's already set. Now, I'm up. Although, Tag has been pretty mysterious lately. But that's his story to tell.

Natalie and I reach the end of the dock where a crew member waits in a tender to ferry us to *Moonbeam*. Like the rest of the crew, he's a member of our pack. He greets us as I help my fated mate onto the craft. We set off, and she looks at me expectantly.

"Um, we're not staying on this, are we?"

I shake my head and point ahead. She follows the direction and gasps.

"Rust! Do you mean that big boat there?"

I nod with a grin.

She blinks and turns back to face *Moonbeam*.

"Seriously? No, way!" My fated mate squeals in gleefully as she claps her hands and bounces again. "I've never been on a boat. This is awesome!"

Then she turns to me with a frown.

"Your pack—"

"*Our* pack," I correct her.

She nods absently and continues, "Owns this boat? I don't mean to sound crass. But how can you afford it? I mean, you're an ER surgeon. No offense."

I chuckle and lean over to kiss her lips, then drag my lips to her ear.

"My pack is known as the *Billionaire Wolves of Miami*. And I'm a billionaire, along with Jagger and several others. I work as an ER surgeon because I want to help people—not for the money. I'm also our pack's doctor," I murmur, then sit back to watch her reaction.

She doesn't disappoint.

Her eyes widen as her mouth drops open. She starts to speak, then stops, and starts again.

I throw my head back and laugh. She pushes my chest and growls.

"What??? Why didn't you tell me??? You're serious, aren't you? I would never have guessed—"

"Damn, you wound me, fated mate! Am I that bad I can't pass for a billionaire?" I ask with a mock sad face and my hand covering my heart.

She giggles then trails off as the tender approaches *Moonbeam*'s stern. Her eyes nearly bug out of her head when she spies the crew on the lower deck waiting to greet us.

They line up in their dress whites. The captain steps forward as the others stand at attention. Jagger selected him for the position since he's a former naval officer who can't get enough of the sea.

"Doc, it's been too long. The ER keeping you from having some fun? Or maybe not," Captain says as the tender slips beside the much larger boat. While the bosun helps secure the tender, Captain reaches out to lift Natalie to the deck. "Welcome aboard, ma'am!" He smiles.

"Thank you," she responds with a giggle as she glances around at the rest of the crew.

"I agree, Captain. It's time for some R&R," I say as I step onto the boat and take my fated mate's hand. My wolf growled at his hands on her, even if polite. "Natalie, this is Captain. Captain, this is Dr. Natalie Moore, my fated mate. She works in the hospital as an OB-GYN."

He tips his hat and turns to introduce her to the rest of the crew. The Chief Stew holds a tray of mimosas. We take flutes with thanks, and I slip my arm around my fated mate's waist.

"We'll get going with the itinerary you submitted. Once we're further out, we'll anchor so you and Natalie can enjoy the watersports," Captain says.

"Great. I'll take her on a tour for now," I respond and guide her up the stairs to the next deck.

As expected, the megayacht amazes her. She oohs and aahs over just about every room, nook, and cranny. We end in an upper cabin just as the megayacht stops. She turns from the windows and points to her sundress.

"Rust, you should have told me we were going somewhere for more than a day's outing. I don't even have a toothbrush, let alone a bathing suit for watersports."

I smirk and stride towards her.

"As you already know from experience if we were alone, you'd walk around naked, including skinny-dipping. But have no fear. I asked Sage to select clothes she thought you'd need, and I ordered your favorite toiletries for you. They're in the closet and in the en suite bathroom."

She throws her arms around my neck. I laugh between her kisses.

"But if you keep this up, you won't leave this cabin," I warn as I nudge her belly with my semi.

"Oh, no you won't! I want to explore all this beauty has to offer. Tonight, you can ravish me. Maybe on that sunbed on the top deck…"

She winks and sashays into the closet. I watch her hips sway and groan as I stride to the en suite bathroom. I'll never get enough of my fated mate.

When I reemerge, she's adjusting the skimpy triangular top of a white string bikini. The piece doesn't even cover the fleshy sides of her lush tits and her ass! What the hell was Sage thinking? I growl and stalk forward.

Natalie jumps, and her tits almost pop out.

"What?" She asks, then rolls her eyes as I tug at the top, trying to stretch it across her tits. She swats my hands away and growls. "Cut it out, Rust! It's a bikini, for goodness sake."

Despite wolf shifters being accustomed to seeing one another naked whenever we shift, I can't help the possessiveness that clouds my mind. She huffs and scoots past me for the door. I grumble as her ass bounces. Fuck! My fated mate is going to kill me.

∽

NATALIE

"RACE YA AROUND THE BOAT!"

I laugh as I zoom on my jet ski past Rust, who's wiping his aviator sunglasses on his board shorts. And boy, does he wear them well. Thick, muscular thighs flex beneath the fabric. His ample package rests between them. Even flaccid, he's magnificent. My mouth waters as I smack my lips. Ummm…

I snap out of my reverie and fishtail the jet ski to splash water all over him. Get him as wet as me. He yells. I hear the revving of his engine and shoot ahead. He gives chase as we fly across the sparkling turquoise surface of the Gulf of Mexico.

We spent the last twelve days cruising along the Florida Keys from Big Pine Key and around Key West. What started as a week-long excursion turns into two. With so much to explore, Rust extended our trip. And I'm beyond excited!

I've never had so much fun, and he treats me like his queen—so attentive in every way. The doubts I had on mating based on the horrible experiences I witnessed fade every day. Rust is nothing like the male wolf shifters of my former pack. He brings me joy and gladdens my heart.

At night, I pretend to sleep so he'll drift off and I can watch him while he's at his most vulnerable. His handsome face relaxes, and he appears boyish. Sometimes, a smile plays at the corners of his full lips. But if I move, his eyebrows knit as he reaches for me with a growl. Even in sleep, he wants to keep hold of me.

If it were two months ago, it would piss me off a male wanted to keep me under his thumb. At least that's how my mind would interpret it then. Now, not so much. It's his way of making sure I'm safe and, of course, close to ravage. Again, something I no longer mind. In fact, I can't wait for him to unleash that anaconda in me. The absolute carnal bliss he bestows on me is beyond mind-blowing. I couldn't deny him, even if I wanted to. I'm addicted to Rust.

So much so, I wonder what it would be like for him to claim me in the age-old manner of our kind. The thought makes my heart soar. I'd given up on having a mate. My expectation was to follow my career path and keep to myself. Now, I see the benefits of having more, of having a mate and a pack.

Rust says he'll introduce me to everyone once we return. I'm nervous as all hell. But he assures me they'll accept me and reminded me of Jagger and Sage's welcoming words. I so hope they're true. If the way *Moonbeam's* crew treats me, it is. The males are friendly but keep their distance since Rust growls whenever they come anywhere near me. The she-wolves go out of their way to make me feel comfortable. I appreciate them all.

As I zoom past the megayacht, the crew cheers with wolf whistles and claps. With Rust gaining on me, I loop around the massive boat. A glance over my shoulder reveals he's right behind me. He whoops and grins as the engine of his jet ski revs. Waves rock mine as he zips past me with a triumphant howl. I growl and pick up speed.

I catch up to him seconds before we reach the megayacht's stern. I throw my head back and howl. He joins in, and the crew's voices rise with ours. My heart lifts with as our glorious melody rises on the wind.

We turn the jet skis over to the deckhands and dive into the crystal-clear water.

It slides over my skin like a warm caress. I luxuriate in the sensations as I channel my inner mermaid. My arms stretch with hands together while my legs press as one to mimic a fish's tail. I flick my feet to propel forward.

Colorful fish swimming amongst the coral below catch my eye. They dart in and around the yellow-green mounds with star shapes on it. During a snorkeling lesson, the deckhand explained it's lobed star coral native to southern Florida and the Caribbean. I give them one last look before I shoot for the surface.

"Gotcha!"

I gasp for air as firm hands grip my waist and propel me from the water. I fly backwards—arms and legs flailing—to drop into the water with a giant splash. Not quite the Little Mermaid…

"Why you!" I splutter as I resurface and swim towards Rust.

He laughs and swims in the opposite direction. His powerful arms and long legs slice through the water with ease. He stops a distance away and spins to face me. He smirks as he dips his head backwards into the water and smooths his shoulder-length hair with his hands. The dark ginger color gleams in the sunlight.

"Come here, Little Girl," he says in a gruff baritone as he crooks his finger.

My eyes flick to the megayacht. It floats in the distance with no crew visible. Since we're the only boat around, I needn't worry about strangers witnessing what I know Rust intends to do to me. However, the idea of someone observing him ravage me clenches my pussy.

As though reading my naughty thoughts, he chuckles devilishly and beckons once more.

Forget the mermaid. I practically run on the water to reach him. My arms go around his neck as he pulls me flush to his body. His mouth descends on mine for a scorching kiss. Tongues twine. Teeth nip. He swallows my mewls as I wrap my legs around his hips.

The anaconda doesn't disappoint. Already thick and long, it prods my pussy entrance. I hump him like a feral she-wolf as I growl with carnal need. My mouth leaves his, and I stare at him with hooded eyes. I purr the words I know will send him over the edge and unleash the savage side of his wolf. I want untamed Rust.

"Fuck me, Rust."

His hazel eyes flash golden as his nostrils flare. A low growl rumbles in his chest. The vibrations skitter over my skin. My nipples bead. So sensitive—even through my bikini top—they rub against the dusting of hair on his chest. I hiss.

He dips his head as he lifts me from the water. His teeth

move the fabric away, and his mouth engulfs a nipple. He suckles. Hard. I throw my head back and moan as my fingernails dig into his wide shoulders. He grunts at the pain but doesn't stop lavishing my breast with sucks, nips, and tugs. His mouth moves to give attention to the other one.

My eager pussy grinds against his eight-pack abs. Even without the water, I would slide along his body, eased by the juices leaking from my core. I lower my head to his.

"Rust, please… I need you inside me."

My swollen nipple pops from his mouth. He tilts his head back to stare up at me. A feral gleam sparks in his wolfish eyes.

"How badly do you need me, Little Girl?"

"*Oh, gods!*" I groan, closing my eyes as his warm velvet voice rolls over me.

A bite to my nipple makes my groan morph into a yelp. My eyes pop open to find him staring at me with a cocked eyebrow.

"So badly," I pant.

"So be it."

He reaches between us and unleashes the anaconda. The slit of his plum-shaped tip winks at me before he uses it to push the gusset of my bikini bottom aside. One upward thrust, and he impales me.

"RUST!"

My scream bounces around us. Surprised seagulls mimic my cry as they take flight. I continue with each toe-curling thrust. Caught in a state of sheer rhapsody, I cling to him, letting him take full control of our carnal pleasure.

His cock swells impossibly bigger. The snug fit triggers another orgasm, and I wail. His grip on my hips tightens painfully sure to leave marks. He buries his face in my neck as he roars through his release. Hot cum bathes my pussy. The walls contract to milk his cock of every last drop of his seed. My mouth opens on a silent wail.

I startle when fangs graze the juncture of my shoulder and neck. The contact ends abruptly as Rust jerks his head away. He stares at me, dismay on his handsome face.

"Sorry. I got carried away," he says in a tortured voice. His fangs glint in the sunlight with the serum male wolf shifters secrete for their claiming bite. I stare at it, mesmerized. But he pulls me away from him.

Our intimate connection breaks.

The loss of his warmth and the disappointment in his eyes make me rethink my demand we wait. Am I doing the right thing by letting my wounded heart dictate my life?

CHAPTER 12

"Are you sure you don't want to join me? We could do a couple's massage or something. I feel bad leaving you while I get pampered."

Natalie scrunches her nose as she scans my face.

It's the last morning of our stay aboard *Moonbeam*. I arranged for an aesthetician and a masseuse to treat her to a spa day while we cruise back to Big Pine Key. They'll give her the works with a body scrub, manicure and pedicure, massage, everything the Chief Stew recommended. Nice, but for a dual purpose. She gets spoiled. Me?

I need a time out.

Three weeks ago, I thought I could withstand the urge to claim my fated mate since we'd be together, and I could seduce her. For a while, the intimacy of sex and shared space satisfied my wolf and me. With her in my arms or on my lap, contentment ran high. I believed she would give in soon. So, I held back.

However, it proves more difficult each time I'm buried in her wet warmth to stop myself from sinking my fangs into her neck to embed my scent in her permanently. The other morning as we fucked in the Gulf and again last night, my fangs descended of their own accord. Serum filled my mouth. I had to wrench my head away and separate us.

The last thing I want to do is claim her without her assent after I promised I wouldn't do it. Not only would it ruin the forward momentum of our relationship. But Sage would have my balls—and cock. I'm pretty damn strong, but I shudder at the thought of losing my junk. Plus, I would lose Natalie and any chance of securing my fated mate.

Then I question whether what I've longed for is worth this torture or not at all. First, her rejection pierced my soul. Now, her ongoing will to deny me claiming her wreaks havoc on my being.

The vision of the male wolf shifter in the Everglades reminds me I don't want to face the madness of not having a mate. It's even worse when the mate is fated and they spend time together. The pain of being apart from Natalie for those three days after she rejected me would seem like a tap compared to the gut-busting punch of absolute denial now. She's embedded under my skin as much as my serum would be under hers—inseparable. It would be like me ripping my own heart out.

I think about Jagger and Dylan. Sure, they had drama with securing their fated mates. But in the end, they made it. Hell, Dylan didn't even believe in fated mates before he met Sasha. He scoffed at the rest of us. Now he's happily mated, and I'm in agony. Fuck!

At this point, I need some advice. I have to talk this shit out with them. Find out what they did and if it will help me with Natalie.

Thus, I keep a straight face as she scans it. While she's in the spa, I plan to call Jagger and Dylan. Gain their perspectives. Help a brother out…

"I'm sure. Besides, you deserve a bit of pampering. Unless, of course, you don't mind a female rubbing all over my naked body with warm oil as she leans her breasts—"

"GRRR! Do *not* finish that sentence, Rust Ingolf!"

Natalie's eyes blaze as she snarls. Her wolf flicks across her features. Fists form at her sides.

Hmmm. Perhaps she does care. Her possessiveness makes my cock harden. But I ignore it. Time out, Rust.

"Well, then, enjoy," I say as I usher her to the cabin's door. "I'll be by the pool."

I drop a kiss on the crown of her head as we part ways at the elevator. She hesitates and glances up at me with her eyebrows drawn together. I spin her around and spank her ass twice. She yelps and hops into the elevator. I wait until the door closes, then jog up the stairs to the pool deck.

I grab a couple of bottles of water from the Viking

built-in beverage center on my way to a sunbed. As I flop down, I pull my mobile from the pocket of my board shorts. I sent a text message earlier, so they expect my call. The FaceTime app rings, and Jagger answers right away. I tell him to hold on while I add Dylan to the video call.

"Okay, so how can we help the Love Doctor?" He asks with a smirk.

Jagger chuckles, then adds, "Oh, don't tease him, D. He called for help, and we'll give it to him without flack."

I nod my thanks to Jagger as I sip from a bottle. Is it too early for aquavit? I sure could use something stronger than water for this conversation. Laughter bubbles from my mouth.

"Private jokes, or what?" Dylan asks with a cocked eyebrow.

"Yeah. On me for having to ask you Mr. Doesn't Believe in Fated Mates for advice on my fated mate. Oh, the irony."

They join in on my laughter. Then Jagger sits up.

"Not all of us can roll around heaven all day. I have a company to run and a meeting in half an hour. So, what's up?"

They listen intently without interruption while I fill them in on my concerns. When I finish, I gulp the rest of the water. Jagger speaks first.

"To answer your question if it's worth the torture, yes. You know the shit Sage and I went through, and it involved more than us. Like Sage, Natalie is an independent female who's used to taking care of herself. Be patient. Imagine coming home to her every night and waking up with her in your arms. I'd walk through Hell for my Sage."

Dylan nods.

"You're right. I denied the truth of fated mates for years. Then I walked into that diner in New York City, and my knees buckled. Me, the toughest of us, MMA cage fighter brought to his knees by a she-wolf a foot shorter than me. When it happens, bro, it happens. And I wouldn't change a damn thing about it. Except for the drama with the fuckers who kidnapped her."

He ends on a growl as his amber eyes flash with his wolf.

I consider their words as I stare at the Florida Keys along the Atlantic Ocean. *Moonbeam* reaches Big Pine Key in a few hours. Back to the cottage for the last week of our alone time. I hope for more. But will accept what Natalie offers so as not to force her. Her reaction to another female with me proves Natalie has grown attached to me. I'll take it as a win.

I thank Jagger and Dylan. We shoot the shit until Jagger's meeting. Before we hang up, they wish me luck. I shake my head.

"Yeah, well, we'll see. If she doesn't give in, I'll go primal and take what's mine."

Jagger shakes his head as Dylan snorts. They know it's all bravado.

Time to cool off. I toss the mobile on the sunbed and yank my t-shirt over my head. I stride to the pool and dive in.

~

NATALIE

"YEAH, *well, we'll see. If she doesn't give in, I'll go primal and take what's mine.*"

Instead of surprising Rust, he surprises me. Tears fill my eyes. I back away from the pool deck and rush for the elevator. Thankfully, it's still there. I slip inside and jab the close button. No way do I want him to see me crying. A sob catches in my throat.

I knew he'd break his promises! It's only been a few weeks, and he's gone back on his word. And here I was about to tell him I was ready for his claiming bite. What a sucker I was for believing in him. He's nothing but a liar!

The door slides open, and I hurry down the hallway for the cabin. My hands swipe my face when I see a stewardess carrying fresh linens in her arms. She raises an eyebrow when she spies my tear-stained face. But I shake my head and rush past her.

"If you need anything, Natalie, let me know. The girls and I are here for you."

Afraid my voice will crack, I wave a hand over my shoulder to thank her. Once inside the cabin, I enter the en suite bathroom to splash cool water on my face. It helps with the redness on my cheeks but not my eyes.

I soak a washcloth in the water and carry it to the bed.

With the pillows fluffed behind me, I lean back and place the cool washcloth over my closed eyes. I push Rust's hurtful words to the corners of my mind and focus on my breathing.

Lips pressed to mine startle me awake. I push against Rust's firm chest as I sit up quickly. The washcloth falls to my lap. I stare down at it not wanting to meet his eyes.

"Whoa, babe! Take it easy. It's me. You almost knocked my front teeth out. How would you like your mate to walk around gumming?"

I ignore his joke. Although it's appealing.

"We're twenty minutes away from Big Pine Key. Otherwise, I would've let you sleep—"

"You can't *let* me do anything!" I snarl as I scooch across the opposite side of the bed away from him. I hop off and stalk to the closet.

I don't want anything from him, including the clothes he bought for me. So, I strip out of the silk caftan and pull my sundress on. It slips past my face, and Rust stands in the doorway.

He frowns as his eye flit over my face.

"What's wrong? Did something happen with the aesthetician and masseuse? I'll let the Chief Stew know."

I growl and push past him. He snags my arm.

"Hey, talk to me. What the hell happened? And what do you mean, I can't let you do anything?"

I snap my head around and glare at his hand on my arm, then at his face and back. He takes the hint and releases his grip. I snatch away and storm for the door. As I open it, it slams shut. Rust's palms press on either side of it, boxing me in. I glare at him over my shoulder.

"Move dammit!"

"No! Tell me what's going on, Natalie."

His lean, muscular body presses all around me. He towers a good nine inches taller. His citrusy, musky, and spicy cologne mixes with his pheromones and saltwater from the pool. The intoxicating combination overwhelms my senses. Rust weakens me.

My forehead leans on the door as I sag.

"Baby…"

He breathes the word into my hair as he drags his nose along my head and down to my shoulder. His knees bend as he presses the fronts of his thighs to the backs of mine. The anaconda unwinds against the crack of my ass.

I bite my tongue to hold in a desperate moan. However, my hips don't get the memo. They undulate to rub my ass along his cock.

"Mmmm… Baaaby…"

My palms slap the door to give me leverage. He has other plans and covers them with his as he entwines our fingers. His teeth nibble at my neck. My knees give out. He groans and braces me with his powerful thighs. The sharp tips of his fangs score my flesh. Warmth drips on the spot. With a throaty moan, my eyes close. I tip my head to give him better access.

"MINE!"

"Rust, Natalie, the tender is ready for you."

The bosun's rap on the door knocks me into reality.

Rust growls viciously. His fingers tighten on mine.

I hear the bosun gulp as he backs away from the door.

"Um, ring Captain when you're ready," he says hurriedly.

"Wait!" I cry and wiggle to free myself from Rust. If I let the bosun get away, Rust will continue with the claiming bite. I won't let it happen, no matter how enthralled I was a moment ago. "Rust, let's go!"

He remains unmoved. I worry he'll go through with like he said. Then he blows a ragged breath and steps back. I sigh in relief and bolt out the door.

The bosun waits at the end of the hallway, as far from the door as possible. He peers past me for Rust. I don't turn around. But I hear him behind me. Judging by the shock on the bosun's face, Rust must look a sight. I sneak a peek.

His narrowed hazel eyes darkened, filled with a feral gleam focus on me. The tips of his fangs dip into his lower lip. Color suffuses his cheeks. A glance at his groin reveals the anaconda standing tall directed at me. A growl rumbles from his chest.

I shudder and swing my gaze forward. The closer I get to the bosun, the more threatening the growl. The bosun flattens himself against the wall and exposes his neck in submission to avoid Rust's wrath. I never thought he would frighten me. But now, I tremble in the face of his need to claim me.

Skirting around the bosun, I head for the elevator. No way do I want to be responsible for Rust attacking him. A wild vision of Rust ripping him from limb to limb flashes in my mind's eye. No way.

It's just a few more feet to the elevator. As much as I want to dash for it, I know better than to run from a predator. So, I keep my pace steady but not quick. The door opens when I press the call button. As I step inside, I glance over my shoulder. Rust bustles in and crowds me in the corner. A sharp cry slips past my lips.

Once again, he brackets me with his arms. His hair hangs in his face as he stares down at me with feverish eyes. His wolf flickers beneath his skin, altering his features. They shift from human to wolf and back again, as though Rust fights for control. His hot breath comes out in huffs.

I stare up at him wide eyed, too afraid to move and risk pushing him over to the feral wolf side.

"Rust, please," I say in a breathless whisper.

He squeezes his eyes shut and shakes his head as if trying to dislodge his wolf's hold. When they open, anguish replaces the wildness. His forehead drops to mine.

"Natalie… What you do to me…"

The elevator door pings open.

"Rust, back out and keep your hands up!"

Captain's commanding words surprise me and piss Rust off. He growls low in his chest. The wolf returns as he swings around to face Captain.

"Stay. Out. Of. This." Rust snarls as his hands form fists at his sides.

"RUST STAND DOWN! NOW!"

Another commanding voice fills the air. Captain holds an iPad in front of him. Jagger—the imposing Alpha of their pack—glares with flashing ice blue eyes from the screen at Rust.

Rust snarls but lifts his hands, unable to withstand his Alpha's command. Rust casts a glance at me.

"ENOUGH, RUST! Go with Captain. Do *not* fuck around. You will not like what will happen to you."

He steps off the elevator and follows Captain, who keeps the iPad trained on Rust. Jagger continues to glare at him.

"Natalie, come with me."

The Chief Stew's voice drags my gaze from Rust. I look at her, and she nods brusquely as she beckons for me to follow.

I glance back at Rust, who's surrounded by every male on the megayacht. My heart sinks. Tears fill my eyes. But I slap them away angrily.

Rust brought this on himself! He's the one who lost control. And do not forget he said he would force you!

I harden my heart once again hurt by a male and follow the Chief Stew. She guides me to a tender where a deckhand waits to transport me to Big Pine Key. I thank the Chief Stew and ask her to give my thanks to the rest of the crew. Without a backward glance, I step onto the tender.

ust

"WHAT THE ACTUAL fuck did you do?!"

Jagger demands as I sit in his office on *Moonbeam*. His ice blue eyes glare at me from the iPad.

Fuck!

I lower my face into my hands. What the actual fuck did I do? I lost control. Fell over the edge. Succumbed to the madness. My worse fear.

All I see is Natalie's stricken face. All I smell is the odor of her fear.

Fuck!!

I don't need Jagger to harp on me. I already regret my actions. What I said I wouldn't do, I did, and worse. She'll probably never want to speak to me again. My heart breaks.

To top it all off, the entire crew witnessed my abysmal behavior. The bosun, worse of all. If he spoke to Natalie—or the gods forbid, touched her—I would have torn him apart. Talk about embarrassing.

And where is Natalie? Is she still aboard or did she leave on the tender?

I need to speak to her. Apologize and let her know I didn't mean to lose it.

"—need to take some time for yourself. Natalie doesn't need to see you right now. You're lucky Sage doesn't realize yet. Well, at least I don't think she does. You would notice. Are your balls still in place?"

I grunt and tune back in to Jagger's words.

"Listen, I admit I was wrong. But you just don't understand. I was about to initiate my claiming bite when the bosun knocked on the door. Damn! I couldn't help myself. I lost my shit," I respond, miserable as all fuck.

Silence descends.

I glance up at the iPad. Jagger stares back at me. He nods in understanding.

"Okay, I get it. However, you scared the shit out of the bosun. Captain said he had peed his pants. I mean damn, Rust. You scared him that bad?"

Now, I feel even worse. Never have I lost control. I'm a Dom, dammit! I thrive on control! Obviously not with my fated mate. Or at least she was.

"I didn't mean it. The urge to claim my fated mate took

control. You've known me all my life. When have I ever lost control?"

Jagger nods.

"Damn. I recognize what that feels like. Sorry, bro. However, as your Alpha speaking, you need to apologize to the crew. As for Natalie, I'll ask Sage to speak with her. As Luna of our pack, she's responsible for the she-wolves," he says, then chuckles. "I'll use my best skills to persuade Sage from shrinking your junk. At least one of us will get something good out of this mess. Any opportunity to ravage my sexy as fuck mate, I'll take it."

I'm happy for Jagger. But my cock and balls shrivel at the thought of Sage enacting her promise. Now that my mind is clear, the magnitude of my error hits hard. He's right, I need to apologize to them. But first to Natalie.

"Listen, I'll apologize to the crew. But first, I need to apologize to Natalie. Talk to her to let her know I didn't mean to lose it. Hopefully, she'll forgive me. I'll call you back after I talk to her."

Jagger stares at me, then shakes his head.

"Natalie left on the tender. You are not to speak to her until after your Luna meets with Natalie. I'll call Sage now and ask if she can use her teleportation magick. She can reach Natalie in seconds. If she says Natalie is receptive to you, then you may speak with her. Do not test me on this, Rust. Best friend or not, I will punish you if you disobey your Alpha's command. Are we clear?"

I BITE BACK A GROWL, knowing he's correct. As Alpha. As my best friend, not so much. But Jagger earned my respect years ago. I will not go against his word.

"Crystal," I respond.

He eyes me a moment, then nods.

"Good. I will reach out once Sage makes her assessment."

He ends the call.

I drop my head into my hands again. How the hell did I let it get this bad?

As I wait for his call, the urge to call Natalie tempts me to ignore Jagger's command. I jump from the sofa and pace around the office. I'm on edge, and my wolf yearns to break free. Suddenly, the walls close in on me. I need air.

With a growl, I stride towards the door. The knob won't turn. Damned if Captain didn't lock my ass in here. Frustration and anger wash over me. I throw my head back and bellow. The sound would surely reach beyond the walls except Jagger's office is soundproof to prevent sensitive information from being overheard. I punch the door and howl in pain. In my ramped up state, I forgot he reinforced the door, ceiling, floor, and walls. His office serves as a safe room. Or in my case, a prison.

I stalk over to the wet bar and grab the bottle of aquavit. Perhaps if I drink all of it, the amount will override my system and dull my emotions. I slump on the couch and tip the bottle to my mouth. Guzzling it down, I finish half of it. Nothing.

I set the bottle aside and pace. Time goes on forever

until at last the iPad rings. I snatch it from the coffee table and accept the FaceTime call. Jagger's grim face appears. My heart sinks.

"Sage spoke with Natalie. She doesn't want to talk to you and asked for you to let her go—"

I hurl the iPad across the office. It hits the wall and shatters to the floor. A gut-wrenching howl rips from my chest. No fucking way! This cannot happen. How could she reject me again?! I know I messed up. But damn not bad enough she wants nothing to do with me. Especially since I told her about the madness.

My mind fractures, and my wolf surges forward. I retreat to allow the feral beast to take over.

NATALIE

ONE MINUTE I'm sitting on the back porch of the cottage bawling my eyes out, and the next Sage appears in front of me. Out of thin air! She scares me so badly my wolf literally jumps out of my skin. But she barely stands before Sage commands I shift. And damned if I don't. Too shocked to speak, I sit here mouth agape until she suggests we go inside and I dress. I glance down, only then remembering my tank top and yoga pants shredded. My mind isn't right.

She follows me inside and sits on the sofa while I

continue to the bedroom. When I reemerge, Sage smiles at me. Her emerald green eyes glow as though lit from within. Their brilliance emphasized by her warm toffee complexion. Curly ebony hair cascades to her waist, cinched by the belt of her silk wrap dress. Long, toned legs —crossed at the knee—end in stilettos. I thought she's stunning on video. But in person, she radiates beauty and power.

"I know my grand entrance startled you. But Jagger wanted me to reach you as quickly as possible."

When I continue to stare at her in shock, she tilts her head.

"Oh, I see. Rust didn't tell you I'm a witch turned wolf shifter. Okay, let's start from the top. And do sit. I won't bite," she says with a giggle. Then continues as I join her on the love seat. "I'm Sage Waters, the High Witch and leader of the Coven of the South. Now, add Larson to my name as I am the fated mate of the Alpha of the Miami Wolves Pack and the Luna. Jagger bestowed me with the gift of wolf shifter when he claimed me. I used my teleportation magick to reach you in seconds. Good?"

I've heard of witches but never met one. And to meet the High Witch, well, damn.

"Good and thank you for the clarification. Rust only told me you and I are the same age," I respond, then shake my head. "You didn't have to come all the way here. I've already told him to let me go."

My voice catches at the end, and I have to cough to clear it.

"Would you care for a bottle of water? I need one," I say as I rise from the love seat. She nods, and I head to the kitchen. When I return, I give her a bottle and continue. "I don't mean to sound rude. I'm sure you're busy and don't need to waste your time."

Sage studies my face as she sips water.

I fidget under her intense scrutiny. Even my wolf tucks her tail and shies away. Just as I open my mouth, Sage speaks.

"You don't mean that, Natalie. Deep in your heart, you know you and Rust belong together. Fated to be one for all time. I understand you're wounded from past emotional trauma. He does, too. But you're a wolf shifter and know how males are single-minded when it comes to their mates. Add being fated, and it's more narrow minded. Wouldn't you agree?"

I consider her words. I can't deny their veracity. However, they don't change my mind. I heard what Rust said about claiming me against my will despite his promise. Then he lost it and would've attacked the bosun! For a male to lose control frightens me. It reminds me of Sam and his cohorts. I shudder and wrap my arms around myself.

No matter what, I must protect my heart. It's had enough heartache to take anymore. My only option is to restart the serum. Hopefully, it blocks Rust from scenting me as his fated mate, and he can go on without madness overtaking him. This last week of my leave of absence gives the serum enough time to suppress my wolf before I return to Miami and the hospital. I'll just avoid the emergency room. Problem solved. Although my wolf throws her head back and howls mournfully. Sorry.

I turn to Sage determined to live my life as I see fit and not conform for a male I cannot trust. Not even one who's my fated mate.

"Yes, I agree with you. However, Rust broke his promise to me. He intended to claim me without my consent. He said so and acted upon it. I cannot trust him. So, please, let me be."

I rise from the love seat. Sage follows and reaches into her handbag.

"Here's my number. You don't have to be alone, Natalie. Call me anytime," she says, then smiles when I take the card. "I will relay your wishes to Jagger, and he will speak with Rust. Now, don't get nervous. I'm leaving the same way I came."

"Thank you, Sage. Know that my intention is not to hurt Rust. My heart comes first."

She nods and lifts her hand in farewell.

I blink, and she's gone.

The room suddenly feels empty, as does my heart.

CHAPTER 14

agger

"Fuck!"

I grab my mobile and pull up the security app. The view of my office on *Moonbeam* appears.

Rust—or rather his wolf—rampages. The massive red beast rakes his razor-like claws on the leather sofa as though gutting prey. Instead of entrails, white stuffing flies around him like puffs of smoke. He snarls and growls with each swipe.

"Dammit, Rust! Stop!"

He pauses and cocks his head at the sound of my voice over the speaker system. For a moment, I think he's going to listen. But no.

He spins, bounds across the office, and leaps onto the large wooden desk. His front leg knocks over the crystal lamp. It shatters on the floor. The pen holder follows the same path. Montblanc and Waterman fountain pens scatter. His claws seek purchase on the polished surface. Trails of scratches appear. Stable, he throws his head back. An ominous howl erupts from his mouth.

His hazel eyes narrow at the camera. The golden flecks glitter as he snarls viciously. Tongue flicks between bared teeth. Ears flatten to his giant head. His stance displays a challenge to my authority as Alpha.

Completely uncharacteristic behavior for Rust. Like Viggo, he's the fun-loving one with a good sense of humor. Sure, he's an Alpha Dom. We all are. But he's not inclined to challenge me as the Alpha of our pack.

No. This outrage comes from hurt. Hell, I know the loss of a fated mate… I get it. But to let his wolf take over. Not acceptable.

"Shift, Rust! Shift. Now!"

I instill my Alpha command into my words and through the bond I share with members of my pack. If this doesn't get through to him, I fear he may have succumbed to the madness. I keep my eyes trained on him through the security camera. It's the best I can do from this distance.

He glares back. Body rigid. His tail wags in a high up position in a show of dominance and aggression. A low growl rumbles in his chest.

Fuck! He won't concede.

With a growl, I slam my fist on the desk. Then switch to the phone app.

"Tag, Rust succumbed to madness… Listen, I don't have time. Meet me in my office now."

I end the call and dial Karl—the head of my personal security and pack enforcers. He enters my office through the door connected to his. A grim expression appears on his face as I recount Rust's madness and show the live feed from the security camera.

Unable to get out, his wolf prowls around the office. Intermittent snarls and growls filter through the speaker. No sign of the man remains. Shaking my head, I turn away from it to alert Captain. He and the crew will leave Rust locked inside until I arrive.

Another call to my pilot to prepare the Larson Enterprises, Inc. Sikorsky S-92 Executive Helicopter.

"What the hell's going on with Rust?"

Tag draws my attention from the mobile screen. I beckon for him to see for himself. He stands gobsmacked.

"Ginny, I'm gone for the day. Reach me on my mobile. Reschedule my appointments," I tell my administrative assistant through the intercom as I jump from my desk chair and head to my private elevator. "Tag, Karl, let's go."

We ride the elevator that connects my office to the garage and to the roof where the helicopter awaits. Karl must have alerted the rest of my security team since they stand beside it. They greet me as Alpha with respective nods while I step aboard. Tag and Karl climb in behind me. Tension fills the luxurious cabin as each of us retreats into ourselves. Concern for Rust and his wellbeing remain at the forefront. His challenge was nothing but the madness. Hopefully, he's not so far gone that I can't pull him back from the abyss.

My fated mate must sense my turmoil. A lightness lifts some of the tension as I answer her call.

"Hi, babe. We're on our way to *Moonbeam*… Tag, Karl, the rest of my team… No! I do not want you to… I know you can take care of yourself. That's not the point. Rust is unpredictable right now… Do not go anywhere near him until I arrive, Sage! Do not push me. Do you understand? Good. I'll see you soon."

"Let me guess, she used her teleportation magick and beat us to the megayacht," Tag says wryly.

I roll my eyes to the heavens with a prayer to the gods for strength. My fated mate wants to kill me. I know it…

I press the intercom built into my seat to ring the pilot to go faster. We zip through the air and arrive in less than forty minutes.

Captain greets me solemnly. I pat him on the shoulder as I jog to my office with the others behind me. I stop in my tracks at the sight of my office door wide open. What the absolute fuck?! I swing my head to face Captain. He shakes his head vehemently.

Tag steps in front of me, followed by Karl and the rest of my security team. I wave them off and push past. This is a delicate situation involving my best friend. No one will interfere. Well, except for…

NATALIE

"OWOOOOO!"

The hairs on the back of my neck rise. I jump from the love seat where I must have fallen asleep. My eyes dart around the cottage's living room in search of the ominous howl. No wolf. I rub the back of my neck as I walk to the back door cautiously. But instead of fear, a sense of loss and pain envelopes me.

I wrap my arms around myself as I peer out the pane of glass. Nothing in the backyard appears out of the ordinary. A glance out the front windows reveals the garden and path clear. I rub my arms as a shiver trails down my spine. Something is very wrong.

As I pad back to the living room, another howl fills my ears. It's not from outside. The menacing cry originates in my head! What the hell?! Again, no fear. Instead, my heart aches. I press my palm to my chest and rub the spot.

I sit on the edge of the love seat and close my eyes. I steady my breath and reach out to the source. In my mind's eye, I see Rust. But not as the man. Rather, a ginormous red wolf.

Its feral eyes focus on me. They narrow, then widen, as if in recognition. *Natalie...* Surprised to hear Rust call my name, I reach my hand out. However, the wildness seeps back into the wolf's glowing golden eyes. It throws its head back and howls before it bolts away out of my reach.

"Rust!"

My eyes snap open and fill with tears. He needs me. Oh, why was I so stuck in my old beliefs? Why couldn't I have given in to what I know I want as much as he does? My gods! What a fool!

I glance around the coffee table, then grab Sage's card. My hands shake as I hold it and pick up my mobile. She answers on the first ring. A second later, she stands before me again.

"Sage, it's Rust! He's lost to his wolf! Please help me get to him. He must still be on the boat. I saw him. He needs me…"

I trail off as another howl fills my head. My eyes close in anguish.

"Natalie, it's imperative you remain calm and in control. I will take you to Rust. But you cannot help him if you are weak. You must be stronger than his wolf to bring Rust back. If not, we may lose him forever to the madness. And Jagger will have no other choice but to—"

"No! Don't say it! I'll do it. I'll be strong. I—I can't lose Rust. I was wrong. This is my fault!"

Sage nods and holds her hand out to me. I grasp it without hesitation.

"Once we reach *Moonbeam*, I will take you to Jagger's office. I can go inside with you—"

"No, I will do it alone. I won't risk your safety for my mistake. Thank you, Sage. Can we go now?"

She nods, and the living room disappears. I blink, and we're in a hallway outside a door on the boat.

"I'll wait here for you. Be strong, Natalie."

I squeeze her hand and turn the knob. They locked the door.

"Hold on," Sage says.

The lock clicks, and the door opens a crack. Sage and I exchange nods, then I step inside, shutting the door behind me. I lean against it. The lock reengages.

The office is in shambles. Stuffing from the furniture is strewn all around the room. Shards of broken glass from liquor bottles, a lamp, and picture frames glitter on the floor. Paintings hang askew on the walls. The acrid stench of urine mingles with musky pheromones and the spilled alcohol. My nose wrinkles as I hold back a gag.

My eyes dart around. But I can't find Rust or the wolf. A low growl catches my attention. I gasp as the red wolf emerges from behind the massive wooden desk opposite the sitting area. As in my vision, its eyes gleam and narrow on me. It moves with the graceful stealth of an apex predator. And I'm its prey. The hairs at my nape lift again, and I shudder.

Be strong, Natalie.

Sage's words sound in my head.

I nod and take a deep breath, ignoring the rancid odor. My wolf paces on the fringes of my being. But I won't let her come forth. The gods only know what Rust's wolf would do if it encountered mine. No. I have to appeal to the man.

"Rust, I know you can hear me. You called to me. And I came—"

A growl cuts off my sentence. Only a few yards separate me from its gaping jaws. Sharp fangs glint from the overhead lights. It continues to stalk towards me.

You can do this, Natalie.

I straighten and lift my chin. My onyx eyes flash with my wolf as I curl my lip. The giant beast hesitates. Its intense stare would make a human lose control of all bodily fluids. But I'm not a human. I am a strong she-wolf, determined to save my fated mate—even from himself.

"Rust! Listen to me. I'm sorry. You're right. I'm wrong. You're my fated mate. We belong together. Forever. Come back to me and make me yours, my love."

The wolf lifts a paw to step forward. I recall Rust's command to me when I launched myself at him in the cottage. My shoulders square, and I stand tall. Glaring at the wolf, I command it.

"SHIFT! NOW!"

Shocked at my boldness, its eyes widen. But its hackles remain raised. Its feathery tail high. Not yet ready to cede domination, it growls.

I issue my own threat as I clench my fists.

"SHIFT! NOW!" I surprise myself with the ferocity of my snarl. Even more so when a sudden crackling and a flash reveal a naked Rust on his hands and knees. His skin ripples as the ginormous wolf retreats beneath it. Rust shakes his head as though dislodging the last vestiges of his beast. Then his eyes lift to mine.

My heart stops.

We stare at one another in amazement.

Slowly, he rises. All magnificent six feet, six inches of sculpted lean muscle in plain view. And an incredibly colossal cock, fully erect and dripping with pre-cum. My pussy clenches, and I mewl as I sag against the door. The need to be strong ebbs from my body, replaced by the need for my fated mate.

His nostrils flare, and he tips his head back to inhale deeply. I know he scents my juices, even above the mess his wolf caused. He rumbles in his chest appreciatively.

My arousal amps at his citrusy, musky, and spicy cologne mixes with his pheromones. My wolf whimpers in need and rolls to her back in submission. I want to join her. I glance at Rust from beneath the thick fringe of my eyelashes.

He approaches with the swagger of an Alpha male about to claim his fated mate. Taut muscles flex in his thighs with each step. The anaconda bobs.

"Natalie…"

The gruffness of his voice sends electric pulses along every nerve in my body. The synapses flash and spark more heat in my already molten core. I whimper in response as my nipples tighten to painful peaks, and my pussy throbs. I rub my thighs together to lessen the ache.

"NO! MINE!"

Rust closes the distance between us in two long strides. One hand grips the back of my neck while the other rips the front of my cotton sundress in one go. It flutters open to reveal my braless breasts. The cool air tightens my sensitive nipples further.

He drops his head and engulfs as much of my breast as his mouth can take, then he draws back to suckle the nipple.

Erotic pleasure zings straight to my core. My fingernails dig into his shoulders as I try to remain upright and not puddle on the floor at his feet. Indecent moans pour from my mouth. My hips undulate, seeking his groin to rub my pussy against for release.

My nipple pops from his mouth. He stands and glares down at me. Displeasure rolls off him in waves.

I gulp.

He spins me around and yanks my hips back. My palms brace against the door. He spanks my exposed ass. A weighty palm lights fire beneath it upon each connection. I dance on my toes, trying to evade his punishment. He bands an arm about my waist and spanks even harder than before.

I cry out. But as the spanking continues, a peace settles over me. I let go, give in to his dominance. His control of my pleasure. The pressure to fight his claiming me recedes giving more space for the peace to flourish. I sigh and hang my head.

He detects the change in me. A few more spanks alternating each ass cheek, and he slows the rhythm. My panting decreases with it as my arousal soars. His palm rests on my ass. My back arches as he leans into me. Warm breath skitters across my ear.

"Do you understand you are mine now and forever, my fated mate?"

My mouth opens to respond. But instead of words, a strangled cry emerges as he slams his engorged cock inside my tight pussy. My arousal eases his passage. However, the stretch burns as my core strains to accommodate his massive girth and length. It hurts oh so good. I cum with legs shaking and knees wobbling.

"Y—Y— Yessss!"

He grunts and pistons his hips. Each thrust drives me onto my toes and ignites the heat in my well-spanked ass. Palms slap the door. Eyes roll to the back of my head as another orgasm rockets through my pussy. My entire body quakes.

"Gods, yes!"

The steady slapping of skin on skin, low and husky growls, and desperate moans reverberate around the office. Sweat trickles down my spine to collect at the small of my back as I arch to take Rust to the depths of my core. The scent of our raw fucking fills my nostrils, and my wolf howls in carnal pleasure.

My pussy walls flutter as the anaconda grows impossibly larger and thicker. The base expands to form his knot, locking us together at the entrance of my core. I scream and writhe at the burn. His free hand snakes around my hip to tug at my clit. Stars explode behind my closed eyelids. I scream his name as my pussy gushes.

A hand swipes the sweat-dampened damp hair stuck to my neck. Then long, tapered fingers enclose my throat like a collar. The other arm tightens its grip around my waist. Warm breath skims across the bared skin at the juncture where my neck meets my shoulder. Hot liquid drips on the sensitive spot. Then pain radiates through me at the same time as his cock floods my pussy with his seed. Blood trickles down my shoulder. I howl from the piercing pain.

Rust increases his holds on my throat and waist as his extended canines coated with his scent serum sink into my delicate tissue. He opens his mouth, then bites the same spot to ensure his scent lodges beneath my skin. He guarantees to mark me as his permanently, with no room for doubt. His head shakes to intensify his claiming bite.

"MINE!"

He growls the singular possessive word, then licks the spot to initiate the healing with his saliva. The rumbling in his chest soothes my cries. Still intimately connected, he lowers to the floor and cradles me on his lap. He buries his face in my hair and murmurs gentle words of love.

I cuddle against him as my eyes drift close.

A kiss to my lips rouses me. My eyelids flutter open to find Rust's handsome face smiling at me.

"Hello, my fated mate. We need to get up. Jagger will be here soon."

The memories of Rust as his menacing wolf, him shifting and claiming me rush through my mind. I return his smile and reach up to cup his cheek.

"Hello, my fated mate. But how do you know?"

He taps the side of his head and grins.

"Our Luna told me."

I giggle, knowing exactly what he means. Then I gasp. "Did she hear us?"

He shakes his head and tells me the office is sound-proof, and she wouldn't eavesdrop on such an intimate act.

I sag in relief. Then wrap my arms around his neck as he lifts me to my feet. I glance down at my torn sundress and arch an eyebrow at him.

At least he has the decency to lower his eyes remorsefully.

"Sage will fix us up," he says, then glances around the office. "And this too, thankfully. I did a bit of damage."

I scoff and lift my sundress for a bit of modesty before Rust opens the door and stands behind it. Sage enters. She scans my face, then Rust. A beatific smiles spreads across her face. She makes no comment about our appearances. Instead, she glances around the office. Within seconds, it's back to its pristine condition. I gasp when a silk caftan covers my freshly washed body and my hair tumbles down my back in glossy waves. A glance at Rust reveals he's spiffy, too. And just in time.

"Sage?! Rust?!"

Jagger bellows as he runs down the hallway. He appears in the doorway. His eyes flit about the office until they settle on Sage. She wiggles her fingers at him. He growls and stalks into the office. Crimson floods her cheeks at the words he murmurs in her ear. Spoken too low for Rust and me to hear. But enough to make her blush and bite her lower lip. A THWACK, and she hops with a yelp. I offer her an empathetic smile as I place a hand on my heated ass.

"Alpha, I apologize for my loss of control. I will apologize to Captain and to the crew, especially to the bosun. Even though Luna repaired the damage I caused, I will accept whatever penance you wish for it and for my behavior."

Rust ends with a bowed head as a show of respect.

But I can't let him shoulder all the blame.

"Alpha, if I may," I start, then continue when he nods in assent. "I will take the majority of the responsibility since Rust reacted to my rejection of him as my fated mate for the third time."

I pause and turn to him.

"I overheard your conversation by the pool. It upset me you would claim me without my consent. Rather than telling you the reason for me rejecting you again, I ran away. From now on, I promise to communicate better and to work on my trust issues."

Rust pulls me to him and lifts my chin.

"I apologize. I said the words out of frustration. Know I would never break a promise to you. However, I understand it from your viewpoint. As for communication and trust, I know just what you need."

A shudder runs through me as he ends with a seductive, low timbre to his voice. I stare into his hooded eyes—

"All right, hold that thought," Jagger says, breaking the sexual thrall Rust cast upon me. "Sage and I accept your apologies. Since your actions were because of madness from the loss of your fated mate, your apology to Captain and to the crew will suffice. Now, why don't you spend the last week aboard *Moonbeam* for your seclusion, then meet the pack in the Everglades? You can complete your mate bonding ceremony, and we'll celebrate with a pack run."

Rust glances at me, and I grin. He kisses my forehead and turns to Jagger to agree.

"I do have a question," I start, then continue when the others turn to me. "I know Sage as a powerful witch can speak to us through our minds. But how was I able to hear the howls of Rust's wolf and him call my name?"

"Our fated mate bond. Even though you rejected me, each time we were intimate, the bond strengthened. My wolf's anger, along with my distress, coursed through the fledgling tether we share. Now that I claimed you, the bond seals our connection. Reach out through it to gauge my emotions."

I close my eyes and cast about until I detect a steady thrum from my heart to his. My wounded heart swells with the love he sends to me. With a joyful smile, I open my eyes and beam at my fated mate. He kisses me softly. We part, laughing at a cough.

"Well, I take it crisis averted?"

A handsome, brawny male wolf shifter an inch taller than Rust stands in the doorway. The newcomer's emerald green eyes flick to each of our faces as he cocks a sable brown eyebrow. Just as with Rust and Jagger, the evidence of their Viking heritage appears in his imposing size.

"Mr. Grumpy! I didn't realize you were here. Allow me to introduce you to my fated mate, Dr. Natalie Moore, now

Ingolf. Natalie meet Tag Dahl, our pack's beta and COO of Larson Enterprises, Inc. One of my best friends."

Tag growls at Rust but smiles at me.

"Problem solved, I'm heading back to the office. Jagger?"

He smirks at Sage.

"I have important business to attend to with my naughty fated mate. I trust you can hold down the fort in my absence."

A grin plays at the corners of Tag's full mouth. He nods and leaves the office with a backward wave.

Jagger and Sage bid us congratulations before they disappear. Her giggles fill the room, then fade with them.

"Ready to be ravaged, my fated mate?"

I loop my arms around Rust's neck to pull him down for a passionate kiss. When we part for breath, I respond with a purr.

"Yes, as long as you promise to give me what I need for communication and trust."

He smirks.

"Oh, Little Girl, we have a special place for that lesson. I will take you when we return to Miami after you meet my parents and the pack in the Everglades. For now, we will make do with what we have available."

An unexpected spank to my ass makes me yelp and jump even as my pussy warms at the thought. I cannot wait for what my fated mate has planned for me.

CHAPTER 15

atalie

"How beautiful! I've heard of the Everglades from nature shows I used to watch with my sister Amanda as pups. But to see it in person and from this height reveals its magnitude and natural splendor. And your pack—"

"*Our* pack, my fated mate."

I giggle at Rust's correction.

A week later and I still forget the Miami Wolves Pack is my new pack. I guess it's because the last seven days of our seclusion, Rust kept me in the cabin. We made love or cuddled in the bed for hours. He fed me on his lap from the tray left outside the door. We bathed or showered, washing each other. At night, we swam naked in the pool, then made love on the deck. I only saw

Captain and the crew as Rust and I disembarked. So, yeah, I kinda forgot about anyone except for my fated mate.

He chuckles when I remind him.

"So, as I was saying… *Our* pack has a camp in the midst of the Everglades. How nice it must be to enjoy the vast amounts of land free of worry humans may see us. As excited as I am to meet everyone and to run as a wolf, I must admit I'm a tad bit out of touch with my other half. It's been so many years I haven't shifted regularly, even before the you know what."

Rust glances at the door that separates us from the flight attendant and pilot aboard the pack's helicopter. Like on *Moonbeam*, they're members of the pack. Rust nods in understanding.

We decided to tell Jagger and Sage about my suppression serum since they're our Alpha and Luna. Rust assures me it's best they know. Plus, Sage may be able to refine it with her magick and definitely secure its safety from the wrong hands.

"I must admit I noticed you were a bit clumsy when you shifted and moved at the cottage when I arrived," he says, then cups my cheek when I pout. "However, there's no need for you to be concerned about your wolf. The connection we have with our other halves doesn't disappear without use. She'll help you the more you shift. And I'll help you relearn our ways. Sound good?"

I turn my head to press a kiss to his palm and nuzzle against it as I purr my agreement.

"Good girl," he murmurs before he slants his mouth over mine.

His tongue coaxes mine to tangle. I lean into him as he swallows my moan. He pulls me onto his lap where the anaconda unwinds beneath my core. I circle my hips to encourage it to come out and play. Rust groans and squeezes my ass cheeks in each hand. He nips my lip, then trails open-mouthed kisses along my jaw and throat. His tongue flicks over his claiming bite, and I mewl.

"Rust, Natalie, we're five minutes from landing."

The disembodied voice of the pilot interrupts us.

Rust growls in frustration and buries his face in my neck. I stroke his hair before I slide from his lap and settle on my seat reluctantly. He entwines our fingers as he leans his head against the sumptuous leather of the cushy chairs.

"I love you, my fated mate," he murmurs with a smile.

I bring our joined hands to my mouth and kiss his knuckles as I stare into his intense hazel eyes.

"I. Love. You. My. Fated. Mate."

I punctuate each word with a kiss, and he grins.

As we land, I glance around the area cleared for a helipad.

"We're near our pack's camp. It's the place we come for pack runs and trainings. For generations, the virtually untouched area of the subtropical wilderness allows us the freedom to be in our wolf form without prying eyes. Over the years, the original pack grounds grew from temporary cloth shelters to simple wooden cabins and now to luxurious residences scattered around the Alpha's house and clubhouse. Glamping—or glamorous camping, as Signy, Jagger's younger sister—calls it. Sage cast a cloaking spell over the entire area for miles as added protection from outsiders.

"A few families and enforcers choose to remain here, not wanting the hustle and bustle of Miami for their principal home. On days like this one, when the humidity is low, the sun sits in a cloudless sky, and fresh air abounds, who can blame them?"

"It's even more amazing on the ground," I say as Rust takes my hand and leads me to an SUV where Jagger and Sage wait for us. I return their waves of greeting.

Sage pulls me in for a hug.

"You're glowing! It must be all that sea air," she says with a wink.

I giggle and respond, "Absolutely, it was relentless!"

We burst out laughing as Rust and Jagger chuckle at Sage's euphemism. Then they herd us into the SUV. I climb in the backseat behind Sage while Rust rides shotgun. Jagger starts the engine. We leave the crew to tend to the helicopter. They'll ride to camp in the other SUV.

Rust points out different spots as we go along. He and Jagger tell stories from their youth about the adventures they and their best friends got into. Sage and I laugh with them. The vision of Rust and Dylan running from hornets after the two hit the nest with rocks on a dare from Viggo brings tears to our eyes.

I smile happily at the thought of meeting Dylan, Viggo —Jagger's younger brother—and the other pack members.

Already, the joy of having a positive pack lightens my heart.

We round a bend and the camp sprawls out before us. Rather, the glamp since every cabin is a rustic mansion of logs and stones in various styles—some ranch and others multilevel, with and without front porches. They surround an open park-like square in the middle, where a lovely garden displays colorful flowers and bushes with wooden benches. Lanes crisscross the land to provide access to the various homes and structures. Members of all ages mill about. Their laughter and conversations fill the air. Content smiles spread across their faces as they interact. Those in wolf form mingle with the others without a care. It's a picturesque village with the incredible Everglades as the backdrop.

I feel right at home.

Sage reaches for my hand and squeezes as she smiles.

"Welcome to our pack's Everglades home, Natalie."

"Indeed, welcome!" Jagger adds as he glances over his shoulder at me. He turns to Rust. "Sage and I figured you wouldn't want to shack up with the bachelors in their lodges, as usual. So, we prepared one of the guest cabins for you and Natalie. If you decide to choose another, let us know."

"Oh, but Natalie, it's the one next to the Alpha's cabin as a place of honor for important guests, and it's decorated nicely. Not that any of the residences lack luxury! I agree with Signy about the glamping!" Sage adds with a giggle.

"I'm sure it's perfect. Thank you both so much! I feel so

welcome already!" I respond as I squeeze her hand and smile at Jagger. "It's been so long since I had family and the love and support of a pack. You make me feel so special."

My voice catches, and Rust spins around on the seat. He leans over and cradles my face between his hands.

"We're your family now, my fated mate. Do not feel sad. And if you do, I will comfort you," he says earnestly. I close my eyes and a tear trickles down my cheek. He smooths it away with his thumb. "I love you, Natalie Ingolf!"

"Speaking of Ingolf… Signy, Sasha, and I put together the overall plan for your mate bonding ceremony. We set it for tomorrow evening. But you have final approval. So, when we get to your cabin, the girls and I intend to whisk you away," Sage says, then glances at Rust with a devilish grin. "Unless, of course, you wish to join us."

His eyes bug, and he flops back onto the seat.

"Uh, hard pass."

I giggle as I dab my face. Sage joins in. Jagger speaks up.

"He couldn't, anyway. The guys and I have plans for our newly mated best friend," he says mysteriously. "A new tradition Dylan came up with."

"No strippers!"

Sage and I shout at the same time.

All four of us bust out laughing. Jagger assures us they would never allow any strippers at their gatherings. Sage and I high five.

Jagger stops in front of an impressive cabin—to say the least. It's a two-story mansion with large river stones around its base and split timber above. Instead of a porch, it has a balcony with a glass wall on the second level that runs the entire length of the front facade. It overlooks the center square. It's more than nice.

We climb out, and Rust scoops me in his arms like a bride. I giggle and wrap my arms around his neck. He strides across the threshold and only puts me on my feet when I protest as Jagger and Sage enter behind us. She takes me on a tour while Rust and Jagger head to the deck off the great room.

Aside from the great room, the home features on the main level a guest bathroom, media room, den, chef's kitchen, and dining room. The second level has four bedroom suites with attached baths. As Sage said, the furnishings are posh but comfortable. I tell Sage it reminds me of a Ralph Lauren home. She laughs and says most of the pieces and accessories come from his home decor collection. I giggle and flop onto a vintage leather chair in the great room. She sits opposite me on the other.

"So, you're happy, then?"

I grin wider than the Cheshire Cat.

"Oh, absolutely! Rust treats me like a queen and loves me beyond measure."

"Good! I won't have to shrivel his family jewels. Now, let's get the girls over to handle business."

We chat while we wait for Signy and Sasha to arrive. I can already tell Sage will be a great friend to me. She's funny, has a mind of her own, and loves deeply. I admire her loyalty to her fated mate, coven, and pack. Their love match was even more complicated than Rust's and mine. Gah!

"Hello!"

"Hey there!"

"Hiya!"

Sage and I glance up to find several members of the pack enter the cabin. An older couple must be Rust's parents since the she-wolf rushes over to me with her arms outstretched. I rise from the chair, and she embraces me.

"My dear! I'm so happy our son found his fated mate. Let me get a good look at you," she says as she holds me at arm's length and inspects me from head to toe. She smiles. "Beautiful and smart! I understand you're a doctor, too."

"Honey, let me welcome her, too," her mate says as he smiles at me. "And yes, Rust did well for himself. I'm his father, Rudolf, and this is his mother, Frigg."

"I certainly did!"

We turn at Rust's voice. He saunters into the great room with Jagger and puts his arms around my shoulders. He leans over and kisses his mother on the cheek and claps his father on the shoulder.

"Well, done, son!"

"So, you're the one who captured Rust's heart?"

A younger, gorgeous she-wolf with waist-length jet black hair and ice blue eyes arches an elegant eyebrow at me. Her cool gaze assesses me. We're the same height at five feet, nine inches. But somehow, she looks down at me. I bristle. Then she throws her head back and laughs.

"And thank the gods! One less *big brother* to hamper my

lifestyle!" She says with warmth in her gaze as she strides towards me. "I'm Signy Larson—Jagger and Viggo's younger sister. Hence their besties adopted kid sister. Ugh! Welcome to our pack!"

I shake her hand as Rust nudges her with a chuckle. She swats him away and sticks her tongue out. He laughs even harder. The rest of us join in.

"And this is Sasha—my fated mate—and I'm Dylan."

It seems as though all the males in this pack are down-right sexy. Golden eyes peer at me from a foot above. I smile and turn my gaze to Sasha. She's an ethereal beauty with ash blonde waist-length hair. Her dove gray eyes sparkle set in an oval-shaped face of alabaster skin. She hugs me with one arm since her pregnant belly makes it impossible for a full embrace.

"Nice to meet you, Natalie," she says in a Russian accent. "I understand you're an OB-GYN. No offense to Rust. But I'd love for you to deliver my baby girl."

"Oh, that's not even a question. No way will Rust continue as your doctor now that we have a capable she-wolf doctor in our pack," Dylan says with a growl.

Everyone laughs at his possessiveness.

"It would be my honor to care for you and your pup. I can tell you don't have much time before you deliver her," I say as I eye Sasha's heavily pregnant belly, then turn to Rust. "I don't imagine you plan for the delivery at the hospital."

He shakes his head.

"No, that's too risky for human interference. We have a

state-of-the-art hospital on the pack's private island, Moon Island, in Biscayne Bay in Miami. And no offense taken, Sasha. In fact, I'm thrilled to pass all the care of the she-wolves to my fated mate. And no, she will not tend to the males!"

Again, everyone laughs.

"What did we miss?"

"Hardy har har."

A male wolf shifter strides into the great room ahead of Tag. I recognize the ice blue eyes from Jagger and Signy and guess he's Viggo. The dark ginger red hair resembles Rust's, but the features match his siblings. Another striking Viking male.

"Viggo! Let me introduce you to Natalie, my fated mate. Natalie, this is Viggo—"

"Jagger and Signy's brother. I recognize the resemblance!" I cut in as I wave at Viggo, then turn to Tag. "Good to see you again, Tag!"

He smiles and nods.

"All righty then. We shall leave you she-wolves to your business. The guys and I are outta here!" Jagger says. He winks at Rust's father and adds, "Care to join us for a bit of mischief?"

The older male chuckles and declines the invitation. He heads out the door with a wave. Rust kisses me breathless and joins his buddies after Jagger and Dylan kiss their fated mates. Signy makes gagging noises while Viggo and Tag roll their eyes. Once they're gone, Sage turns to me.

"Now, let's get started."

"ENOUGH WITH THE fancy mansions for the Everglades! Time for us to get back to the male style and rough it. No built-in espresso machines. Don't even start me on the steam showers. Forget about the manicured lawns. We're leaving it all behind from now until noon tomorrow. Get changed and grab your packs, fellas. We're out!"

Viggo glances at me. I turn to Tag. He cocks an eyebrow at Jagger, who snorts.

"For real? D., what the hell do you have planned exactly?"

"Since we're bonding ourselves to our fated mates one by one, I figure we should renew our best friends' bond each time one of us pairs up. Remind ourselves we got each other's backs. No male left behind type of attitude."

We express our agreement, then a feral gleam lights his golden eyes as he chuckles wickedly and rubs his hands together.

"Now for the good part… We hike to the spot we used to hang out at as pups. Pitch tents. Hunt as wolves. Explore. I arranged a few activities for us, including airboat races and fishing. So, if you're finished asking questions, let's. Get. At. It!"

Pumped up, he claps his hands for emphasis.

"Yeah! Let's do this, like Brutus!" Viggo exclaims as he fist bumps with Dylan. Then they throw their heads back and howl.

Jagger, Tag, and I glance at each other, then join in their call. It reverberates around Dylan's great room. My heart soars with it, excited to spend time with my boys. We end with exploding fist bumps and change into the new gear Dylan laid out for us—tank tops, cargo pants, socks, and heavy boots. The packs slip onto our backs before we head out.

"We each have a satellite phone in our packs. So, you won't be completely disconnected from the world, you wusses," Dylan adds as we tromp along the path headed for the tree line.

As we pass beneath the pine trees, I send a blast of love through the tether Natalie and I share. I grin as my heart swells with her response. Being with my boys is great. But nothing beats my fated mate.

"Rust! You're back! I missed you, baby! How was your Guys' Getaway?"

Natalie jumps to her feet from where she sits on a chaise lounge and races across the deck, arms outstretched. She stops abruptly a few feet away and wrinkles her nose.

"Um… You're stinky. What did you guys get into? Or what didn't you get into? Ewww!"

"Oh, no, Jagger! Don't even think about—"

Sage squeals as he dips his shoulder into her belly and lifts her onto his shoulder. Her long hair tumbles from the bun. Curls bounce as he jogs past Natalie and me. Sage's giggles trail behind them.

I turn my hungry gaze on my fated mate. She lifts her hands up, palms out, as she backs away from me, shaking her head. I growl low in my chest. She shudders visibly as her pupils dilate. The outline of her plump nipples appears beneath the thin cotton tank top. The tip of her tongue darts out to moisten her lips.

"Rust…"

Her sultry purr causes blood to rush to my already thickening cock in the confines of the cargo pants.

Twenty-four hours for Dylan's rugged adventure prove too long of a separation from my fated mate. I'm hungry for her. Stinky or otherwise. Her backing away only triggers my hunting instinct. The predator in me howls, eager for the chase.

Natalie must sense my mood through our bond. Her

hooded eyes widen before she spins and scampers towards the other end of the deck. I watch in appreciation as her ass in skimpy shorts jounces with each hurried step. I allow her a head start, then howl as I pursue her through the glass accordion doors. She shrieks and runs for the stairs. I lope after her.

"Rust! Our mate bonding ceremony is in a few hours! You can't just ravage me now! Oh!"

I swipe her calf as she races up the stairs. She catches her balance on the banister and rushes on.

"You're incorrigible, Rust Ingolf!"

I chase her all the way to our bedroom suite. She peeks over her shoulder as she flings our suite's double doors open. I growl. She hops like the frightened hare my wolf devoured last night. Now, it's her turn.

Before she reaches the bedroom's doors, I lunge forward and grab her by the waist. She sails through the air and lands on the bed. She scrambles to her hands and knees. The silky curtain of her midnight hair covers her beautiful face.

But it's her perfectly round ass that draws my attention. I allow my claws to extend and drag one from her ankle and up her inner thigh, leaving a trail of goosebumps in its wake. Her legs quiver as she moans and drops to her forearms, forehead on the bed. The position elevates her ass, and I rumble in approval.

The claw drags along the gusset of the minuscule shorts to trace her folds. A line of moisture appears on the white linen. She arches her back with a throaty moan. Her ass rises higher. I lick my lips, greedy for a taste of her honey.

The claw slips beneath the gusset. She gasps as it scoops some from her dripping pussy. I suck on the claw and growl. She shudders from the animalistic sound. Her whimpers increase my desire to devour her.

With one swipe, the claw rends the shorts in two. The pieces flutter to the bed as she gasps. The claw retracts, and my hands grip her hips. I lower my mouth to lap straight from the fount. Her body convulses as I force orgasm after orgasm from her pussy. Her honey gushes into my mouth. I swallow it down with satisfied grunts.

I reach for the zipper of my cargo pants. She cries out at the sound of the teeth parting. I fist the base of my cock, then slam home in one brutal thrust. It sinks within her wet heat to bottom out at her womb. My groin cradles her ass while my heavy balls slap her engorged clit. I grunt when her pussy walls clamp on my cock like a vise.

She moans and tosses her head as her pussy stretches to accommodate my girth. To ease the burn, my thumb and index finger slip beneath the hood of her clit to tease the sensitive nub. She bows her back as her pussy juices gush on my fingers and drips between her knees. Her natural lubricant coats my cock.

I grip her hips and pummel her pussy. The insistent need to fuck her outweighs gentle lovemaking. Our bodies smack together in a carnal rhythm. Her desperate moans mingle with my hungry growls. The air around us explodes with the musky scent of sex and sweat.

It's a quick and dirty fucking. A few thrusts, and I go off like a geyser. Hot seed shoots into her womb. A savage roar punches the air. Sated, I collapse on top of her, flattening her body to the mattress. She bears my weight with a throaty moan.

*N*ATALIE

"Y*OU LOOK GORGEOUS,* N*ATALIE.*"

"You don't need any makeup. That glow outdoes any blush!"

"So pretty."

"Rust will fall in love with you all over again."

Through the trifold mirror in the bedroom's sitting room, I smile tearily at the girls and his mom. Sage rearranged the room for my mate bonding ceremony preparation space. A rolling rack of exquisite dresses stands to the side with shoes and sandals arranged below it. Lace and silk lingerie rests on a dressing table. Champagne bottles sit in a sterling silver bucket with crystal flutes and strawberries on the coffee table. It's wonderful except it's missing my Mom and Amanda.

Signy hands me a tissue with a smile.

"I know you must miss your family, especially today. We can never erase your pain or replace your sister and mother. But we adopt you into our pack and our circle of girlfriends. You have us, now, Natalie."

The others gather around me for a hug. The sadness in my heart lifts, and I smile with happiness.

"Thank you. It means so much to me."

A knock at the door followed by Rust's father's voice.

"May I come in?"

Frigg unlocks the door, and he smiles at her as he strides in the sitting room. He stops a few feet from me. His smile widens.

"Natalie, how lovely you are," he says, then continues after I thank him. "It would be my honor to walk you to the ceremony bower."

Once again, tears fill my eyes. I nod, unable to verbalize a response.

"Now, we can't have you all weepy as you greet your fated mate. Allow me?"

I turn to Sage and nod. She grins and works her magick. Immediately, the tears stop and my cheeks dry. A rush of elation sweeps through me. I giggle and thank her.

"Shall we?"

I slip my arm through Rudolf's.

The girls and Frigg bustle out ahead of us. We get into the golf carts and make our way to the open, park-like square.

Amidst the garden and benches stand rows of long rectangular tables with white tablecloths and white wooden chairs. Floral arrangements line the center with buckets of Champagne. Chafing dishes with a variety of foods and beverages sit on tables to the side. A separate table holds a four-tiered cake. Columns of intertwined tree branches and flowers strung with thousands of fairy lights surround the area to allow for the celebration to continue after the sun sets. A ceremony bower with the same treatment stands at one end. I smile at the magickal fairy-tale, all thanks to Sage.

The pack gathers in front of the bower while Rust waits beneath it with Jagger. Sage slips from the first golf cart and circles the pack to stand opposite Rust and Jagger. He grins at her. But Rust only has eyes for me.

He looks up the aisle as I alight from the second golf cart. Our eyes connect. His glow with a love so fierce, my heart skips a beat. A pulse reaches through our tether. I smile brightly at my fated mate as Rudolf escorts me down the aisle. Rust strides towards us, nods at his father, and scoops me into his arms. I giggle and wrap my arms around his neck. The pack wolf whistles and claps. He turns for the bower and settles me on my feet.

"Natalie Moore, I claim you as my fated mate to protect, love, and cherish for all time. To bear my pups and to stand by my side. I love you, Natalie Ingolf, my fated mate!"

I swallow back tears of joy, then clear my throat to respond.

"Rust Ingolf, I claim you as my fated mate to protect, love, and cherish for all time. To bear your pups and to stand by your side. I love you, Rust Ingolf, my fated mate!"

More shouts and howls of rejoicing fill the air.

Rust scoops me up and swings me around. My head goes back as I howl with joy. He joins me for a song of love. Then he carries me back up the aisle as the pack congratulates us. We settle at the head table with Jagger, Sage, Rudolf, Frigg, Viggo, Tag, Dylan, and Sasha. Once everyone takes their seats, Jagger and Sage stand with flutes of Champagne.

"It is my great pleasure to welcome Natalie Ingolf as the fated mate of Rust Ingolf to our Miami Wolves Pack—"

Cheers interrupt him. He waits with a grin for them to finish.

"Natalie is an OB-GYN and will assume the role of doctor for all she-wolves—"

The males clap and stomp their feet. Jagger chuckles. He and Sage raise their flutes.

"Tonight, we celebrate Rust and Natalie's mate bonding with good food and fellowship, followed by a pack run. Join Sage and me in welcoming Natalie to our pack!"

I laugh as the space rings with the howls of dozens of wolf shifters. Rust grips the back of my neck and kisses me passionately. More howls and whistles fill the air.

"Now, let us feast!"

Jagger says, then he and Sage sit.

During dinner, every member of the pack introduces themselves and offers well wishes. Their heart-felt welcome gladdens me. Nerves flitter away with the breeze. I lean against Rust, and he tucks me against his side.

"You take my breath away, my fated mate," he says as he places a kiss on my temple. "How are you doing?"

"Thank you, my fated mate. Marvelous, darling! Simply marvelous."

He chuckles and kisses the tip of my nose.

I sigh, content to be held and loved so dearly.

We eat, drink, and dance as the sun sets. Soon, the pack grows restless, ready for our run. Jagger senses the change in mood from festive to eager. He rises and announces the start of the pack run. Everyone strips where they stand and shifts amidst crackles and flashes.

As I slip out of my dress and sandals, I glance at Rust, who stands naked. Only the wolf paws on his sculpted pecs cover his divine body. He smiles encouragingly.

"I've got you, babe. Your wolf has you, too. Now, shift."

My body follows his command. In seconds, I'm on four paws. I lift my gaze to him. He winks and shifts. My wolf purrs at the sight of his massive brown wolf. He approaches and nuzzles my throat. My body vibrates at his touch. He rumbles deep in his chest, then throws his head back and howls.

Soon the sultry Everglades' night resounds with the howls of dozens of wolf shifters. Leaves rustle as creatures of the night hasten to their lairs to avoid the apex predators on the loose. A barred owl hoots as it takes to the air wings flapping to reach the sky. In the distance, a Florida panther yowls to remind us how cats hate dogs before it too slinks away. The hum of winged insects remains as a backdrop to our calls. The pack makes its presence known and silences the rest of the wetland.

Above, the waxing gibbous moon signals redirection,

adjustment, and flexibility. I take it as a sign for new beginnings with my fated mate and my new pack. I'll relearn my wolf with his help. And I will let go of the rigidity caused by my wounded heart. It's time for healing.

I throw my head back and howl.

Around me, the pack stamps their paws and rejoins my call. I revel in the camaraderie and am as eager as they to sprint through the saw grass marshes and pine flat woods. Jagger and Sage set off. His giant silvery white wolf and her smaller ebony one rush for the tree line. Rust nudges my flank, and we follow. I match his pace. Shoulder to shoulder, we run together. Our paws land with each step silently.

The invigorating run heightens my senses. My body tingles as the wind ruffles the dense coat of my midnight and white streaked fur. My eyes adjust to the darkness. The landscape appears as though daylight reveals it. Scents of the Everglades inhabitants fill my nose. At once, I feel carefree.

Along the way, Rust romps and teases me affectionately. I respond with yips and barks. Excitement sparks in the air around us.

Miles later, we rest on our haunches. I take the time to familiarize myself with the new surroundings. Several members pair off and separate from the pack. Rust nudges me and rises. He darts away, and I give chase. We reach a cluster of dense pine trees. He moves beneath the low hanging branches. Inside, a patch of ground covered in pine needles makes the perfect hideaway.

He turns to me and rumbles. I quiver with need as he approaches. Without prelude, he mounts me. I howl and paw the ground with my front feet. He takes me with feral growls. My slick eases his savage thrusts. His front legs tighten around me as the base of his cock expands to form his knot.

I whimper as my pussy contracts. More than our mate bond, we lock together physically. His hot seed fills my core as he howls. I join his carnal song.

While we remain as one, he rumbles to soothe me. Once his knot deflates, we separate. I whimper and rub my body against his before I curl up on the bed of pine needles. He lies beside me as my eyes drift closed.

My last thought of how happy I am for what's to come makes me purr.

ust

"YOU KNOW, a she-wolf could get used to this swanky lifestyle."

I chuckle at my fated mate as she waggles her eyebrows seated beside me in the helicopter.

We just lifted off with Jagger, Sage, Dylan, Sasha, Tag, Viggo, and Signy. The rest of the pack members—including my parents—fly in other helicopters or drive back to their Miami residences. Everyone was excited about the pack's newest addition. Over breakfast, several members told me how happy they were I found my fated mate, who could care for me as I have for everyone else. I couldn't agree more.

Especially as I grin at her now.

"Well, get used to it, babe. I plan to spoil you rotten!"

Everyone laughs.

Jagger pulls his mobile from his pocket and accepts a call. He puts it on speaker since it's from Magnus—Alpha of the Los Angeles Wolves Pack.

Natalie reaches for my hand as she stares at the mobile like it's a rattlesnake set to strike. I squeeze her hand reassuringly. She nods.

"Hello, Alpha, I have you on speaker with my Luna, beta, Natalie, Rust, and my most close confidantes. What news do you have for us?"

"Hello, Alpha. Good and bad."

Natalie gasps as her eyes widen. I pull her onto my lap and rumble to soothe her distress.

"Give us the bad first."

"That Sam is a wily fucker. He escaped my enforcers by squirreling down some hidden hole he has beneath the floorboards of his house. It took them a few days. But they found him hiding out with a pregnant she-wolf. The female was more than happy to be rid of him."

"Well, thank fuck!" Jagger says. "But if him being captured is the bad news, what's good?"

Magnus chuckles.

"My head enforcer met his fated mate! I gave him my blessing as the pack's new Alpha. He'll have the rest sorted out quickly."

"Excellent—"

"Uh, excuse me, Alpha," Natalie says, then continues when Jagger nods. "What happened to Sam?"

Magnus growls.

"The dumbass thought he could challenge the new Alpha. And got his throat ripped out."

Natalie sags with relief, then asks, "Would you and the new Alpha mind if I visited the pack? I would like to visit my family's graves and check on the she-wolves."

"Absolutely! Let me know when you and Rust want to come. I'll arrange everything for you. And my congratulations on your mating."

We thank him, and Jagger ends the call. All eyes turn to my fated mate.

"Thank you. You do not know how much this means to me. A peace I haven't had for many years settles over me. I truly appreciate your kindness."

She bows her head humbly.

"You're welcome, Natalie. Your wellbeing—as with the rest of our pack—is Sage's and my top priority. We do whatever we can to help."

My fated mate nods, too overcome for words. I rock her in my arms and nuzzle the top of her head. She buries her face in my neck. After a while, she calms and returns to her seat with a smile.

I point out landmarks as we fly to distract her from any sadness and to remind her of her new home and family. She thrills at the coastline and vastness of the Atlantic Ocean. I tell her we'll go swimming on South Beach. Soon, Miami's skyline comes into view. The pilot takes us along the barrier island to give my fated mate a bird's-eye view of the city.

When we land atop the beachfront building on Ocean Drive where the bachelors live, she stares out the window in awe. Viggo and I hop out. I turn around and help her from the helicopter and grab our bags. We bid the others goodbye before we leave the rooftop for the elevators.

"So, we have a new resident. A she-wolf at that, huh?" Viggo asks.

I shake my head and respond, "Not for long. I'm no bachelor, and my fated mate needs a residence. One she can make our own."

"Where will we go?" She asks as we board the elevator.

"I have a bayfront plot on Moon Island near Jagger and Sage and Dylan and Sasha. I'll take you there after I put our things away here. We can build a residence to your liking."

Her eyes widen as her mouth opens and closes a few times. I place my index finger beneath her chin to draw her mouth closer, then slant mine over it.

Viggo groans. I chuckle and slip my arm around my fated mate's waist when the elevator doors open on my penthouse floor. Mine is the highest in the forty-story building with Viggo's next in age order. Natalie waves goodbye, and we step into the entry foyer.

"If the entry is fabulous, I can't wait to see the interior!" She quips as she glances around the space where two glass and steel tables with bouquets of white flowers flank steel double doors etched with wolves.

I smirk as I press my palm to the plate, then push the doors open. I drop our bags inside. With a flourish, I scoop her into my arms bridal style and carry her over the threshold. Her giggles morph into oohs and aahs as the Atlantic Ocean comes into view through a wall of windows across the expansive living room.

"My goodness, Rust! This is spectacular!"

She wiggles to get down, then rushes to the glass wall as soon as her feet touch the white marble floor. I follow and wrap my arms around her as she stands gaping at the unobstructed view.

Two cruise ships on the horizon and several megayachts float on the turquoise water. A person on a parasail powered by a speedboat flies by in the clear blue sky. Higher still, a plane displays an advertisement banner for a luxury condo. I chuckle when I see it's one of Larson Enterprises, Inc's new properties. I point it out to my fated mate, and she shakes her head in amazement at all of it.

"Are you sure we want to move? I mean, this place is phenomenal, and I haven't even seen the rest of it!"

I'm a possessive fucker. The idea of my fated mate riding the elevator with the male wolf shifters of our pack makes my wolf snarl and bare his fangs. Nope. Not happening.

"Sorry, babe. I will not allow the horny bachelors of the pack to ogle you on a daily basis. Do you want me to go feral, or what?"

She giggles and nudges me with her elbow.

"Are you a wolf or a caveman, Rust Ingolf?"

I bend down to press my lips to the delicate shell of her ear and murmur, "I'm a possessive male who will protect his fated mate at all costs."

She shudders, and I chuckle wickedly.

"Come, I'll give you a tour since it'll be a few months before our residence on Moon Island will be ready. You have until then to enjoy the penthouse. If that's a consolation for you."

She shakes her head but takes my hand.

We finish the tour in our bedroom suite. Her laughter and comments end as she stares at the king-size bed. I frown.

"What's the matter?"

She nibbles on her lower lip as her eyes flick between the bed and me. I shrug and raise my eyebrows.

"Um… I love the room. But… um… I don't want to sound like a prude or anything. But the bed. I'd rather not sleep where you had sex with other females. Sorry. Not sorry."

I chuckle, and her brows knit as she turns away. I rush behind her and grab her by the waist.

"Are you jealous, my fated mate?" I croon in her ear.

She pushes at my hands. I hold tighter.

"Now, you know what I would feel if we stayed here amongst all these males," I say, then continue when she stills. "However, other than my mother, no female has ever entered my residence. You are the only and the last lover to writhe beneath me in my bed. Do you understand?"

I finish on a growl with a thrust of my hips. Her jealousy makes my cock instantly hard.

She mewls a breathless yes.

"Now, let us make good use of *our* bed."

NATALIE

"OKAY, now, a James Bond car! What will you shock me with next?" I ask as Rust leads me to something straight off the big screen in the posh action-packed movies.

"Oh, my fated mate, it only gets better. Just you wait."

I slip inside as he holds the door open. It's so low, I almost fall in! He reaches over and pulls the safety belt across me. Then places a kiss on my lips before he strides around the front and slides into the driver's seat. I roll my eyes at how easily he made it.

We're on our way to Moon Island. He'll show me around our pack's private island and take me to the plot for our new home. I'm so excited, I bounce on the luxurious leather seat. I turn my gaze out the window. People in other vehicles stare at the car—rather Bugatti La Voiture Noire, as Rust told me. I can't blame them. It's a masterpiece. They can't see me through the tinted glass, but I smile anyway.

We zip along MacArthur Causeway, leaving South Beach behind. More cruise ships docked at the Port of Miami await passengers. Their sheer size makes me wonder how the ships remain afloat. Soon, we turn off the causeway and pull up to intricate wrought-iron gates. Rust tells me they're the entrance to Moon Island. Two members of the security team sit in the guardhouse. They recognize Rust's car and wave.

He lowers his window and returns the gesture. I lean over and tell them hello. They greet me with warm smiles.

The gates' swing inward as the sensor detects its counterpart installed in the car. We drive through and along what Rust points out as the main road. He points out more sights as we drive along the entire island.

Homes ranging from ranch style to two- and three-story line the road. Some front Biscayne Bay, while others have interior views. On the other end, in the interior of Moon Island, a mini town offers options for those who prefer not to leave our protected land. A school for younger members of the pack, restaurant, deli, pizza shop, beauty salon, and barber shop are available.

The wealth of our pack continues to astound me. Never would I have imagined I would be in a situation like this one. I chalked my life up to being single and working hard at my career. Now, I have a fated mate who dotes on me and a new practice as the doctor for the she-wolves of our pack. Thankfully, Rust promised he won't force me to stop my work at the hospital or to have pups right away. I shake my head unbelievably. Now, I consider having pups even if not now. I guess that's what love and security will do for me.

As we pass a driveway covered in stone pavers leading to a Spanish-style ginormous mansion, Rust tells me it's Sage and Jagger's home. Okay, wow. I press my nose to the window as I try to get a good look at it. Rust chuckles and says we can call and see if they're up for a visit after we go to our plot nearby. I nod enthusiastically.

"That's Tag's residence next door. And this, my fated mate, is our plot set on Biscayne Bay, with direct water access. The acreage will allow for a home as large as Jagger and Sage's residence. We have a few architects and interior designers in the pack. I worked with two of them for the South Beach penthouse. Come on, we can walk the land so you can get a feel for it."

He hops out and helps me from the supercar.

I tilt my head back and let the glorious Miami sun shine on my face. A deep inhale brings the scent of saltwater and fragrant gardenia and jasmine flowers to my nose. Paradise!

Rust leads me to the edge of the property where mature palm trees rise tall and flowering bushes grow on the grass lawn. It extends uninterrupted from the road to the bay. Birds chirp in the palm fronds and bees buzz around the bushes. It's extraordinary.

"What do you think? Can you envision us here with a palatial home and room for our pups to run and play? Once you're ready, that is."

I rise on tiptoe and cup the back of his neck to bring his face closer to mine. I rub the tip of my nose against his, then press our foreheads together.

"I can envision it and so much more. When can we meet with the design team?"

"Hello, there, Rust and Natalie!"

Surprised, I turn to find a male wolf shifter and a she-wolf approaching us. They wave. I wave back, then lift an eyebrow at Rust. He grins.

"How about now?"

I laugh. My fated mate wastes no time!

A short while later, they leave with a follow-up meeting set in a few days. They'll present their ideas and sketches. I gave some input but can't wait to see what they come up with since they know the Miami style better than me.

Once they're gone, Rust takes my hand and leads me to the water's edge. He cups my face and stares at me with so much love, I feel it through our mate bond. I return it twice fold. I love my fated mate!

He pulls a small navy blue suede box from his jeans pocket and opens it.

My heart skips a beat.

Nestled in silk, a giant diamond ring sparkles in the sunlight. Rainbows glint off its flawless surface. I guess the oval-cut diamond is at least fifteen carats and set in platinum, with smaller round diamonds on the band. Unbelievable.

"I would have given you your wedding ring at our mate bonding ceremony. But it wasn't ready, and I didn't want to rush the custom piece. I selected an oval cut to match the shape of your gorgeous face," my fated mate says as he lifts the ring from the box and takes my left hand. He slips it on my ring finger as he continues. "Now, with my claiming bite on your neck and my ring on your finger, no one can wonder whether you are mine, Natalie Ingolf."

He lifts my hand to his lips and kisses it.

Tears blur my vision.

He rumbles deep in his chest and pulls me into his arms. I nuzzle my cheek against his heart, relishing its steady beat. One that only beats for me.

"Now that we handled the details for our new home, I will fulfill my promise to teach you to communicate better and to trust me. I told you I know just what you need. Tonight, I will show you, Little Girl."

CHAPTER 18

 ust

"W HAT'S ALL THIS?"

My fated mate stops and stares at the gift boxes on our bed as she adjusts the towel wrapped around her freshly showered body. She approaches the bed. Her fingertips glide over the glossy black wrapping paper and matching bows. Her eyebrow arches as she glances at me over her shoulder.

I cross the floor and plant a kiss on the bare flesh as an arm bands around her waist. The other hand tugs the towel. It drapes down her body. I cup a full tit and brush the pebbled nipple with my thumb. She moans, and I tweak the sensitive bud.

"Gifts for you, Little Girl."

I skim my fingers down the flat plane of her belly and cup her bare mons. My fingers delve between her wet folds to tease her swollen clit. Her head falls back against my shoulder as her hips gyrate. She bleats when my fingers spank her pussy.

"Be still. Now, open them."

I step away to watch her reaction to the erotic presents. My erect cock throbs in anticipation beneath my black leathers. I stroke the bulge languidly. Soon it will fill her wet warmth.

She touches each box, then decides on the smallest one. The bow slips free to the floor, followed by the discarded wrapping paper. The top lifts. She pushes the black tissue paper aside. Her eyes widen as she holds up the strands of pearls and black silk ribbons to her throat.

"Oh, Rust! This is gorgeous! Thank you, my love!" She gushes as she turns to me with a bright smile.

I chuckle and shake my head as I take the pearls from her hand.

"You're welcome. But the piece is not a necklace. Here, I will put it on you properly. Widen your stance."

She frowns but does as I command.

Standing behind her, I loosen the silk bows and slide the portion shaped like a triangle between her thighs and hold it to her mons. The double strand of pearls slips between her ass cheeks. She gasps as they glide along both sides of her clit and stroke her back entrance—which I will claim soon. I re-tie the bows at her hips.

"That's how you wear your pearl thong, Little Girl," I

say in a voice roughened with carnal lust. Then slap each ass cheek. I groan as they jiggle enticingly. I add two more for sheer pleasure. She mewls and shimmies her hips.

"Next gift, Little Girl."

She takes a deep breath. A startled gasp slips from her parted lips as the pearls work their magic. Wide eyes peek at me over her shoulder as she hesitates.

I reach over and spank her ass in quick succession.

"When I tell you to do something, you do it naughty girl," I admonish.

"Y—Yes, Rust," she stutters.

"We will discuss more details in a moment. But you will call me Sir when we play—not Rust. Do you understand?"

"Yes, Sir."

Her cheeks flush crimson as she bites her lower lip.

Fuck. Me.

My cock leaks with pre-cum.

She turns to the bed and surveys the gift boxes. The rectangular one catches her eye. She removes the ribbon and top. A pair of six-inch, black marabou mules emerge. She blinks.

"Uh, Sir, they're fabulous. But I've never worn heels so high."

I take the mules and crouch before her. A tap to her calf, and she lifts her foot. I slip one on, then repeat for the other. I press kisses to her thighs, mons, belly, and to each nipple as I rise. Now, she stands three inches shorter than me. My erect cock nudges her lower belly. Perfect. As I expected.

Her pupils dilate.

"Do you trust me?"

She nods.

I clasp her chin between my thumb and index finger.

"Words, Little Girl. I will have your words."

She blinks, but responds, "Yes, Sir."

"There's my good girl. Next."

She bites her lip and spins around, then gasps as the pearls and my cock arouse her further.

I remain behind her as she bends over to reach the largest box. My fingers skim her hips. Tugs to each silk ribbon presses the pearls closer to her clit and puckered hole. She moans and bucks with a mini orgasm. The scent of her arousal wafts into my nostrils. I growl.

Her hands tremble as she opens the box.

Beneath the tissue paper lies an exquisite hand-crafted black corset with pearls. The sculpting design creates an hourglass figure with lace panels across the front in a butterfly shape and nipped in at the waist with a narrow strip of velvet. Elastic trim crisscrosses to form the shoulder straps, center panel, and outer panels of the lace.

She lifts it with an awed expression on her face.

"Astounding," she breathes.

"Here, I will help you."

Deftly, I place the corset on her and adjust it for a perfect fit. A bow around her neck and tiny ones between her amble tits lifted just right and at above the pearl thong make her look like a present. My present.

I step back. My mouth curves into a devilish smile as I

twirl my finger for her to spin. She blushes but keeps her glittering onyx eyes on mine, glancing over her shoulders with each rotation. My feral grin spreads. My wolf howls.

"Come, Little Girl, or we will never reach our destination," I command as I rip the wrapping paper from the last box and remove a black Burberry trench coat. She slips her arms through the sleeves. I place my arm around her waist to keep her steady in the fuck-me mules. "Now, we go."

We ride the elevator down to the garage and slide into my one of my supercars. She remains quiet during the short ride along Ocean Drive. But the sexual tension is palpable as she fidgets in her seat and my cock throbs in my leathers. The musky aroma of her arousal fills the supercar's interior.

I guide the supercar into a driveway directly across from the Atlantic Ocean in a South Beach historic, beachfront gated mansion. She glances through the windshield, then out her tinted window.

"Where are we?" She asks as she squints at the discreet gold plaque with to Club Sol & Mani Miami written in a script font.

Cole—the club's valet and a young wolf shifter—opens her door.

"Good evening, Rust, Natalie."

"Good evening," we respond in unison.

She giggles as she takes his hand and rises from the low supercar. I growl at him for touching my fated mate. He raises his hands palms out and rounds the back of the supercar. She offers him an apologetic smile as I place my hand on the small of her back and usher her to the side. Laughter from members as they frolic in the mosaic-tiled pool within the sun-filled courtyard floats in the balmy evening air.

"Welcome to Club Sol & Mani Miami the luxury, members-only club owned by our pack."

She frowns and glances down at herself, then back at me with an arched eyebrow.

"If you think I'm going dancing in this risqué outfit, you have another think coming, mister!"

I hold back a chuckle and put on my stern Dom face.

"Oh, naughty girl. You will learn to trust me. All the more reason tonight's lesson is so important," I say. She lowers her eyes. "The club provides a safe space for those in the BDSM lifestyle. And as you know, I am a Dominant. You, my Little Girl, are a submissive."

Her eyes jump to my face as her mouth opens to protest. I place a finger on her lips and shake my head.

"You will give in to your submissive nature. I will guide you as your Dom—a highly skilled Dom. You display all the signs of a sub. You will recognize and appreciate them under my guidance. Now, come the night promises much pleasure."

We enter the club through the scrolled wrought-iron and glass doors.

"Good evening, Rust, Natalie. Enjoy," the doorman says with a smile.

We pass him and enter the opulent lobby where two she-wolf greeters stand behind a podium.

"Hello, Rust and Natalie!" They chorus cheerfully. "We're so excited for you! We'll take your coat, Natalie. Go right in."

She smiles at them, then glances at me questioningly. I untie the trench coat belt and unbutton it. Her lips part. I cock an eyebrow. She takes a deep breath and relaxes. I slip the trench coat off and hand it to the greeters.

A couple enters behind us.

My fated mate balks and places her hands over her ass. I rub her arms until she settles, then place my hand on the small of her back. I increase pressure to urge her through the double doors behind the greeters.

We enter Exhibition where demonstrations and performance rooms provide entertainment—or inspiration. The Dungeon provides a spacious section devoted to public forms of BDSM play. Those not in the lifestyle may think it's a medieval dungeon for torture with the St. Andrew's Crosses, spanking benches, chains suspended from the ceiling, and more. To those who enjoy the lifestyle, the pieces and assorted whips, floggers, canes, and implements are to be expected.

Which is why I chuckle when she gasps and freezes. Her wide eyes dart about Exhibition, taking in the sights. Four male wolf shifters surround a she-wolf spread out on a leather padded table. Her hands and mouth work three cocks while the fourth plunges in and out of her pussy. She moans and writhes in ecstasy. A she-wolf sits on her calves bound by red silks artfully arranged by a male wolf shifter trained in Shibari. Other demonstrations range about the space. The sounds of carnal pleasure and the scent of sex mixed with heightened pheromones blend for a hedonistic atmosphere.

"This way, Little Girl," I murmur in her ear.

She wobbles unsteadily by the distractions. I tighten my hold and lead her to a secluded area.

"What are Sage, Jagger, and the others doing here? They're Doms and subs too? Is this a party?"

"You'll also learn to stop thinking so much and go with the moment, Little Girl."

We stop where the others gather. Jagger and Sage greet us along with Dylan, Sasha, Viggo, and Tag.

"Your corset is fabulous, Natalie!" Signy exclaims, then winks at me. "Nice choice, Rust. You did well!"

"Thank you. I love your lingerie set. I just wish I knew what was going on," my fated mate responds, and glances at me.

I spank her ass, and she yelps.

"Unless you want to perform our collaring ceremony with a heated, red bottom that matches the soles of your mules, I suggest you remember what I just told you about thinking, naughty girl."

"Yes, Sir."

"Good girl," I praise her, then continue. "Our friends gather to celebrate our union as Dominant and submissive."

Jagger holds a navy blue suede flat box for me. I press the cabochon clasp to open the lid.

A custom-made collar rests on the silk lining. Tiny

sparkly diamonds cover the intricate platinum lacework of the three-inch wide collar and the lock. I lift the delicate piece and place it around my fated mate's neck. The soft click of the closure makes my cock pulse. Mine!

"Natalie, I give you my collar as a sign of my love and my vow to teach you communication and trust. My collar always shows your status as a partnered sub—my sub. You will obey me in all sexual interactions unless you want all play to end with the use of your safeword, *red*. For a Dominant to place a collar on a submissive equals the pair's commitment to their D/s relationship. On some levels just as important as a wedding ring is to a marriage. I have never collared a sub. Only you. Do you understand, Little Girl?"

Tears fill her eyes. She opens her mouth to respond but can only nod.

I lean over and brush my lips over hers as I murmur words to settle her.

"Yes, Sir." She responds with determination as she traces her fingertips lightly over the exquisite craftsmanship of my collar, then rests them on mine.

My heart swells with pride. My cock swells with carnal lust.

The others clap. Sage, Signy, and Sasha hug my fated mate while my best friends clap me on the back. They're Doms and understand the significance of the collaring ceremony.

A pulse of need rushes to my heart over the tether. I turn to find my fated mate surrounded by her friends. Yet her eyes focus on me. I nod and return her message with a strong one of my own. Her lips part on a gasp.

"Well, fellas, my sub has need of her Dom. Thank you for witnessing our ceremony. Good night!"

They chuckle as I prowl towards my Little Girl to take her to my private suite upstairs. Sage, Signy, and Sasha scatter at my presence, chattering like little birds. I bend and dip my shoulder into my sub's belly to lift her onto my shoulder. She squeals, and I spank both ass cheeks, cupping one to hold the fire inside. She gives in and hangs submissively.

Yeah, she's a natural sub. And it will be my absolute carnal pleasure to draw her into my BDSM lifestyle.

atalie

"Natalie! Sasha is in labor! Can you come to Moon Island's hospital now?"

Dylan's panicked voice sounds through my mobile as I leave the day's last patient in an exam room at the OB-GYN department.

It's been a week since I last saw Sasha and Dylan at Club Sol & Mani Miami. I thought then she seemed close to delivery. But she assured me she was fine and still moving about with ease. Well, things change!

"Absolutely! I'll be right there—"

"Go to the hospital's roof. I sent the helicopter for you. He'll be there in five minutes... It's okay baby, Natalie is on her way… Ten minutes, that's all, baby. Don't worry. Listen, Nat, I have to go to Sasha. See you soon."

While he spoke, I ran to my office and grabbed my bag. On the way past the receptionists' desk, I tell them I'm gone for the day. Miraculously, the elevator arrives in less than a minute. I burst out on the highest floor, then race up the stairs to the rooftop. As I fling the doors open, the helicopter lands. The flight attendant opens the door and waves me forward. I hop in, and we lift off.

I pull my mobile from my pocket and send a text message to Rust since he's in the emergency room until eleven tonight. Before I put it away, the three dots indicate his response. Dylan already told him, and he'll come after his shift ends.

I glance out the window for signs of the Moon Island hospital. As Rust told me, it's a state-of-the-art facility with all the latest equipment and two operating rooms. They spared no expense to make it the best care facility for our pack. Departments include urgent care, general medicine, obstetrics, and pediatrics. It's rare a wolf shifter requires medical assistance since we have enhanced healing. But accidents can happen that require further help. The most used department being obstetrics.

Over the last week, Rust gave me a tour and introduced me to the staff of nurses, aides, and the head of administration. They expressed their excitement about a female doctor on staff. I set up my office and exam rooms. I met with the midwives for lunch. They shared their knowledge and told me which she-wolves were expecting and which hoped to conceive. I scheduled appointments with each of them. Their mates were relieved and thanked me profusely. So, I'm all set to help Sasha.

The pilot announces our arrival. I jump from the seat and hop out the moment the flight attendant opens the door. We landed on the front lawn, making it easy for me to rush inside and to the obstetrics department.

I round the corner and see Signy, Jagger, Tag, and Viggo in front of Sasha's delivery room.

"Nat! Thank goodness! Sage is in the room with Sasha, Dylan, and the midwife. Sasha doesn't want magickal help —silly girl! So, hurry!" Signy says as she waves her hands.

"When did she start? Do you know the time between her contractions?" I ask rapid-fire questions as I rush past them.

"Three hours ago, we were eating ice cream, and she complained of a stomachache—"

"Obviously, she was mistaken!" Jagger chimes in.

I nod and push through the door.

"Oh, thank the Fates!" Sage exclaims as she rises from the chair beside Sasha's bed. "Tell me what you need. I'll help without my magick."

I nod and speak to Sasha as I wash my hands and switch to a fresh white coat.

"How do you feel?"

"Oooo… Like I'm going to *castrate* my fated mate!"

Dylan shudders and bows his head.

I bite my lower lip to keep from laughing out loud. The

midwife catches my eye and smiles. Then she catches me up on Sasha's vitals. I check her cervix.

"You're not far now, Sasha. I want you to focus on your pup being in your arms soon and how much love you and Dylan have for her. Can you do that for me?"

Her dove gray eyes focus on me. For a moment, I think she's going to curse me in Russian. But she nods quickly and closes her eyes. Dylan presses a cool compress to her forehead. She opens her eyes and smiles softly at him. He sighs and leans over to kiss her lips.

My heart pangs. I turn away from their tender moment. Am I ready for pups now? What would it be like to be in Sasha's place with Rust pampering as best he can between me snapping at him? Sasha's sharp cry pulls me from my musings.

"Let's have another look, Sasha."

I check her again. Not much change. I tell her we'll have to wait a bit longer, and she growls. Dylan widens his eyes. It's comical to see the fierce MMA fighter scared of his she-wolf fated mate. Poor thing.

My mobile vibrates in my pocket. I glance at Sasha. She leans against the pillows propped behind her back with her eyes closed. Good. I shift my gaze to the mobile screen and smile as I open the text message app.

Hi, babe. How's Sasha? Better yet, how's D.?

My grin widens. He knows his best friend so well. My fingers fly across the screen as I type my response.

She's good. Not much longer to go. D.... He's another story. I hope he doesn't faint! I'll keep you posted. xoxo Your Heart

"I'll go tell the others it'll be a while," Sage says and leaves the room.

I check Sasha's and the pup's vitals. All sounds and appears as expected. She's young and won't have an arduous labor. And since it's her first delivery, it will take longer. But less time than human females. She-wolves deliver faster.

While we wait, I make certain the station for checking the baby after birth along with the bassinet, diapers, blankets, and bedding are prepared. As my fingertips brush the soft cotton, my mind drifts back to the thoughts of me giving birth to Rust's pup. Would we have a female or male? Does he prefer one over the other?

Since he told me he won't force me to have pups right away, he hasn't mentioned a family of our own. He focuses on the two of us. The trips he plans to take me on—like the one to tour the major European cities, including Paris, Milan, Rome, Amsterdam and up to the UK for London and Glasgow. We'll go once I get more time at the hospital. On our days off, we'll go to the Bahamas or back to the Florida Keys. That's exciting. But what if—

"NATALIE! Get this pup out of me!"

I hurry to Sasha's side and place a hand on her round belly. The pup shifted. I check her cervix, and she's ready. I tell her we're good to start with pushing, and she nods, biting her lip. Dylan stares at me in shock. I smile at him encouragingly. He needs more help than Sasha. I nod at the midwife, and we settle in to deliver their pup.

Thirty minutes later, Inessa Vang makes her glorious

debut. Sasha says her name is Russian for pure and symbolic for her and Dylan's love. Tears fill my eyes as they do his at her pronouncement. The midwife and I leave the new family to bond. We go to the waiting room to tell the others who wait anxiously for news. Everyone cheers. Jagger congratulates me on a successful delivery. I smile and thank my Alpha and my friend.

After a while, Dylan enters the waiting room to tell us he and Sasha want to introduce the pack's latest member. We rise and follow the proud papa. I send a text message to Rust, then put him on FaceTime so he can take part in the introduction. Dylan holds his tiny pup to his massive chest and announces her name, Inessa Vang. Her eyes blink open to reveal amber eyes like her sire. We cheer. They thank me for delivering their pup and the midwife for her support before we leave the room.

Sage invites me to dinner with her and Jagger. I tell them I'll meet them at their home after I write my notes in my office. Once alone, I let my mind wander to a family with my fated mate.

Maybe the time is closer than I thought.

EPILOGUE

hree Months Later
Rust

"Congratulations on a fantastic property!"

"Damn, bro, you went all out, huh?! Well done!"

Natalie and I stand on the rear lawn of our newly finished bayfront residence on Moon Island. We invited our pack to the housewarming. And I have to agree. The architect and designer captured the modern Miami style Natalie and I want for our home. She loves the style of our former penthouse and wanted it on a larger scale.

The two-story glass and concrete mansion has five en suite bedrooms, two bathrooms, an open floor plan living, dining, and kitchen, media room, family room, gym, infinity edge pool and spa, pool house on the terrace with an outdoor kitchen, and so much more. Manicured lawns in the front and the rear with flowering bushes and palm trees make for a lush landscape. South Beach and the Atlantic Ocean beyond create a spectacular backdrop.

We just moved in yesterday, and already it feels like home. The only things missing are little pups running around getting into everything. Since Sasha gave birth to Inessa, I can't stop thinking about my fated mate and I having pups of our own. Dylan strides around with a puffed chest and shows pictures of his little pup every chance he gets. Then there's Jagger with his twin pups, Harald and Tove. He's no better than Dylan. I don't blame them. I'd do the exact same thing.

I shrug to myself and smile down at my fated mate. She's happy, and that's all that matters to me. My world is complete with her in it. Pups would add more joy. But I won't push the topic. Instead, I'll have patience. When the time is right, we'll have a family of our own.

"Rust? Did you hear me?"

I blink and shake my head.

"Sorry babe. I was in another world. What did you say?"

Her onyx eyes scan my face, then she smiles.

"Sage asked about a nursery."

My heart skips a beat. I cock my head to the side and stare at my fated mate.

"I told her we don't have one."

My heart sinks. But I manage to keep a straight face. I turn to Sage and smile.

"Yeah, we won't need one for a while. We have plenty of

time. For now, we're enjoying one another. We have trips planned and fun to be had at Club Sol & Mani Miami. We're good for now."

I ignore the look Jagger sends my way. I don't want to go any further down that path. Instead, I excuse myself and head to the outdoor kitchen where Viggo mans the Viking grill. At least the bachelor for life—as he refers to himself—won't mention pups or nurseries.

"Hey, bro. I've got some burgers ready. You want one? Well, actually, you look like you could use some aquavit."

He turns to the wet bar behind him and pours a two-finger tumbler for me. I thank him and sip it as I watch him plate my burger.

"You know, you could earn a decent living as a cook," I tease.

He rolls his eyes and shoves the plate at me. Then dings an imaginary bell.

"Order, pick up!"

We laugh.

I take a seat at the oval table and smile at the pack members seated around it. My mate bond tether makes me glance up. Natalie walks towards me with a smile. I grin back. Her hair flows behind her, caught by the breeze. The colorful silk maxi dress skims her curves. She looks radiant. I shift in my seat to adjust my burgeoning erection at the sight of my gorgeous fated mate. We may not have pups. But we certainly put in enough practice.

She greets the others at the table, then leans over and wraps her arms around my neck.

"Hey, good looking, what you got cooking?" She asks with a giggle.

I lift the burger to her mouth, and she takes a hearty bite. Her moan makes my cock jump.

"Wow, Viggo knows what he's doing with a grill!" She says after she swallows.

I nod in agreement as I pull her onto my lap. I alternate feeding her and myself until the burger disappears from the plate.

We chat with the others, then mingle with those milling about the property. When the sun sets, the fireworks display begins. The brilliant sparklers light up the sky above Biscayne Bay. Everyone oohs and aahs in delight. The pups of other members laugh and point at each burst of color. I smile at their excitement.

Later that night, my fated mate and I sit on the balcony off our bedroom suite on the second floor, overlooking the bay and ocean. We reflect on the day and how happy we are with our new home. She climbs into my lap to straddle my thighs and nuzzles her cheek against mine.

"I love you so much, Rust Ingolf."

"I love you more, Natalie Ingolf."

"But some things are missing from our life, and I'm not happy about it."

I sit up straight, concerned, and stare at her.

"What—"

She places a finger on my lips and smiles. Leaning to my ear, she continues.

"I want lots of pups with you, Rust Ingolf. A little pack of our very own. Now, *Sir!*"

THANK you for reading *Rust The Rejected: A Wolf Shifter Rejected Mate Paranormal Romance*!

If you enjoyed the book, I would so appreciate your review as they make a huge difference for indie authors. Be sure to sign up for my newsletter for the latest info about the series, new releases, and a FREE book at**bit.ly/ CLBooksDylanTheRogue**! Next up: *Tag The Redemption: A Wolf Shifter Fated Mates Paranormal Romance.* Turn the page for a preview.

PREVIEW TAG THE REDEMPTION: A WOLF SHIFTER FATED MATES PARANORMAL ROMANCE

ag

"AND THAT CONCLUDES the marketing department's promotion plan for the new build in Naples."

A hush descends in the conference room as fifteen pairs of eyes peek nervously at me. I keep mine laser focused on the male wolf shifter who heads the marketing team for the Naples residential project. He lowers his gaze respectfully as he awaits my comments.

As the COO of Larson Enterprises, Inc. it's my responsibility to manage and to handle the day-to-day business operations of the Miami Wolves Pack's multibillion-dollar company. Including working closely with department heads and supervisors to support the daily activity of employees.

A lot of pieces must move in sync to maintain Larson Enterprises as the top company in the hospitality industry for luxury hotels, fine dining, clubs, and lounges. Founded in Miami by our pack Alpha's family—with Jagger Larson as the current CEO. I'm his second in command as COO and as his pack beta. Both roles I take very seriously.

So much so that I will not tolerate less than stellar work by staff. And that means I have to hold back an irritated growl at the half-ass "promotion plan" presented. I'm surprised the male bothered. He should have known better. And I don't hesitate to express my dissatisfaction. At. All. They don't whisper I'm a bosshole for nothing…

"Do you truly expect me to believe you did your research, Jackson?!" I bark, then hold up my hand when he opens his mouth to respond. "Rhetorical question. Obviously you did *not*. Otherwise, you would recall a similar 'promotion plan' presented three months ago. One I rejected. The same I do with this one. You have twenty-four hours. I expect an *original* plan on my desk."

"Yes, Mr. Dahl, sir," he responds, then slinks to his seat.

As he hovers above it with his hands on the armrests, I shake my head with several tsks. His startled eyes jump to mine. I cock my head.

"Don't you think you should gather your team now? You have your work cut out for you, Jackson."

He stutters a response as he hops up and dashes towards the double doors.

I watch him go, then flick my gaze to the head of business development.

"Sally."

The human female swallows audibly, bobbing her head as she rises.

"Yes, Mr. Dahl, sir."

I sit forward, lean my elbows on the sleek conference table, and steeple my fingers. Next...

Two hours later, I stride past the staff on the executive floor on my way to my suite of offices. We employ wolf shifters and humans. Best for our kind to hide in plain sight and all. Although we've been here a hell of a lot longer than the humans.

Several millennia ago, Scandinavian Viking wolf shifters sailed from the Old World and landed along the East Coast of what's now the United States. The six packs headed by best friends who sought new lands moved throughout the continent to form territories, with ours settling here. We maintain close ties with our brethren through friendship, mating, and business. Plus, our Ruling Council gatherings keep us informed of happenings throughout the packs.

Our Miami Wolves Pack is the most powerful pack in the South. Because of the success of Larson Enterprises, other packs refer to us as the *Billionaire Wolves of Miami*. Further reason for me to ensure I fulfill my responsibility to take Jagger's CEO vision for the company and turn it into an executable business plan. Correction, a *flawless* executable business plan. So, call me bosshole all day. And sometimes all night.

I round the corner to my office suite and nod at my

administrative assistant, Beth. The she-wolf scampers to her feet from behind her desk outside my office and hands a file folder to me. Her head tilts back since I tower over her at six feet seven inches.

"Here's your speech for the charity gala tonight, Mr. Dahl. Communications made your requested edits, sir."

"Thank you, Beth. My date is aware of the time I'll pick her up?"

"Yes, Mr. Dahl. I spoke with Katrina an hour ago. She confirms she will be ready. Your lunch delivery is on its way up now. Both Mr. Larsons, Dr. Ingolf, and Mr. Vang wait in your office. "

I figured as much since the opaque treatment blocks the clear glass wall. Jagger must have activated it knowing we'd want privacy for our weekly Guys' Lunch. Today it's my turn. Naturally, I'm hosting it here in between meetings.

More than likely, I'll hear about it from them since I'm always in the office. So what? Unlike Jagger and Dylan, I don't have—nor do I want—a mate that keeps me tethered to her side. Or like Viggo, who can't stay out of any female's panties. Rust is the only one as tied to his job as I am to mine. He's in the emergency room as a critical care surgeon more than anyplace else. Inwardly, I shrug. Outwardly, I nod at my assistant.

"Thank you, Beth. You may leave for your lunch early."

"Thank you, Mr. Dahl."

I open the double doors of my office. My best friends lounge on the white leather sofa and chairs in the sitting area with their feet up on the coffee table and armrests guffawing. Thank the gods my office is obscured and soundproof with this lot.

We've been friends since we were pups. My father Branson was the enforcer for the former Alpha Marcus—Jagger's father. Jagger and I were born a few weeks apart and inseparable for twenty-eight years. My mother Ylva teases the former Luna Sigrid she stole her only pup. Rust Ingolf and Dylan Vang are a year older, while Viggo came along three years later as Jagger's younger brother. The five of us share a strong bond as best friends, even going so far as to get wolf paw tattoos on our pecs. Well, Jagger wussed out, claiming he has no interest in marring his perfect body. Regardless, we treat each other like blood brothers. And that includes getting on my nerves kicking back on my furniture with no care whatsoever...

"Hello, gentlemen. A pleasure, as always."

They pivot as one pack. Heads cock. Eyes sharp. Nostrils flare. Then the grins spread across their faces, laughing at the scowl on my face as my eyes flick between their feet and the furniture.

"Why hello there, Mr. Grumpy!"

"How's your grumpilicious day going, bro?"

"Why the sour face? Don't you love us anymore?"

"I hope your status meeting went better than the expression on your face..."

I shake my head as I loosen my silk Hermès tie and shrug out of my bespoke Saville Row suit jacket. Oh, yeah, we're all billionaires, and they're dressed in similar high-end apparel. Young, sexy AF, and wealthy beyond our wildest dreams.

"Hello, again. My day would be better without your boots on my white leather sofa. I can't get rid of you, so I'm forced to love you. Other than a wreck of a promo plan, the meeting went well, surprisingly."

A knock on the door cuts into their uproarious chuckles. I stride over and open it. Beth leads the delivery person to the conference table beside the floor-to-ceiling wall of windows.

As they arrange the gourmet meals from a Larson restaurant at each chair, I glance at the view always captivated by the stunning panorama. The Larson Tower stands across from Biscayne Bay. Beyond its azure waters—where jet skiers zip by and megayachts cruise along—lies the Atlantic Ocean. Its dazzling turquoise surface extends to the horizon as far as the eye can see. I inhale and relax. The clamoring of the guys as they pull out chairs and check who has what food interrupts my all too brief respite. I roll my eyes and drop into a white leather executive chair.

We shoot the shit about the latest Miami Dolphins football game, Viggo's new blinged out watch, and our upcoming deep-sea fishing trip to the Bahamas. My mobile vibrates in my pocket. I groan at the photos on the screen.

"What's up?" Rust asks as he peers over my shoulder. He barks out a laugh. "For real? You've gotta be kidding me!"

He snatches my mobile and passes it to Dylan, who guffaws and passes it to Viggo and on to Jagger. Until I grab it back with a growl, emerald green eyes flash with my displeased wolf.

"What the hell is Katrina up to?"

I sigh and run my fingers through the short length of my sable brown hair.

"She's accompanying me to the charity gala tonight. I thought she behaved well at the hotel opening last week and figured she'd be a suitable candidate for another social event. Obviously, she thought more of the invitation."

Dylan chuckles and smirks.

"You don't say? If the lingerie pick under the guise of 'Which do you prefer?' didn't clue you in, I don't know what would!"

I groan and respond with a terse not interested and no need to get dressed at all since you won't join me, then toss my mobile on the table.

Viggo studies me with ice blue eyes so like his brother's but has dark ginger red hair like Rust. I cock my head at the younger wolf shifter.

"Why don't you hire another assistant who can manage your social calendar and attend events with you? As an employee, she won't expect to become Mrs. Tag Dahl. Better yet, hire a human female. Then it's zero chance of her thinking she's your mate. We may fuck a human female. But it's been decades since a male wolf shifter turned a human in our pack. No wrong ideas or vavavavoom photos!"

He snaps his fingers and sits back, arms crossed over his muscular chest. A triumphant grin appears on his face.

I stare at him.

A human female assistant to handle my personal affairs with no endgame to mate with me? No coy smiles or hair flips? Actual conversations and not double entendres? A business professional who expects a paycheck and not a diamond rock? Well, damn! Let me contact Human Resources right now.

A grin spreads across my face as the idea settles in.

"Hell yeah, Viggo! That's just what I need. In fact, I'm emailing the head of HR—"

My mobile skitters across the smooth surface of the table like a hockey puck. Dylan's massive mitts catch it as he grins at Jagger.

"Not now, you're not. You're having lunch with your best friends. Work can wait," Jagger says with a smirk. "And I'm telling you that as Alpha, CEO, and best friend. No room for dispute or negotiation, bro."

I roll my eyes and sit back.

These guys are lucky I do love them. Or else I'd kick their asses.

"Now that you dumped Katrina, who will you take?"

I shrug in answer to Rust's question.

After seeing the she-wolf's unwanted photos, I'd rather go alone. Although, having a female on my arm keeps others at bay. Well, for the most part. I've had a few approach me the moment my date stepped away to the ladies' room. I may be a bosshole. But I'm still a gentleman and made it clear I was with someone. Tonight, I won't be in the mood to dodge hopeful females.

"Take Signy. The social princess is always up for an event if her calendar allows a last-minute engagement. Give her a reason to wear one of her beloved haute couture gowns."

Viggo's suggestion pulls me from my musings. His and Jagger's younger sister is the pack princess and a little sister to me. So, again, no chance for mistaken expectations. Perfect!

"Damn, bro, you're on fire today, huh?" Dylan teases with a smirk. "Trying to get Brownie points or what?"

Viggo throws a handful of French fries across the table in response. Herbs and Parmesan cheese crumbles drop to the surface. Dylan picks the fries up and pops them in his mouth.

I growl, and they laugh.

"Listen, I'm not due to the ER for another few hours. I have no interest in saving either of your asses from Tag's wrath. So, cut the shit," Rust says as he eyes them.

Dylan grabs him in a headlock and nuggies his head.

I refuse to play referee—or preschool teacher—and ignore them. Instead, I snag my mobile to call Signy.

***

"It never ceases to amaze me how well you scrub up. I remember you as a pup chasing behind your brothers and the guys to prove you're just as tough."

Signy rolls her ice blue eyes as I tease her.

She's a gorgeous she-wolf and dressed spectacularly in a signature red Valentino haute couture gown with a matching clutch and strappy stilettos. Her waist-long ebony hair piled atop her head in an easy bun and blood red lipstick offer contrast to the elegant gown. Ruby and diamonds sparkle on her ears, neck, finger, and at both wrists. An absolute stunner.

Which is exactly why her brothers and the rest of us run interference with any male who dares to get close to Signy. Only the best and the most worthy male will court the pack princess. At twenty-four, she has plenty of time before she mates. Not that she has a choice. Especially since Jagger nixed the attempt by an Alpha from out west to claim her.

"Tag, that was decades ago! Now, come on or, we'll be late, Mr. I Have an Overseas Call I Can't Skip."

She loops her arm through mine and drags me towards the front doors of the bayfront mansion she lives in with her parents. I help her into the back of my chauffeured Bentley Bentayga and round the back to slide in beside her. An enforcer for the pack serves as my driver and personal security, along with a second enforcer who rides in the passenger seat.

She bleeds my ear about her latest exploits—social events attended, philanthropic work—pack gossip, and her next trip to Europe for fashion week. I indulge her like a good older brother, even though my mind drifts to my business trip.

"—And the cow jumped over the moon."

I frown and lift an eyebrow at her. She shakes her head.

"You weren't listening to a word I said, Tag. Let me guess, you have some important business on your mind?"

I open my mouth to protest, but she lifts her hand to stop me.

"That's why you need to take a hint from your boys and find your fated mate. Then you won't only have Larson Enterprises to occupy your mind."

Thankfully, the luxury SUV stops in front of the Larson Miami Hotel & Resort, saving me from responding. Without a word, I hop out and stride around to her side. The enforcer holds her door open while I extend my arm. She places a dainty hand on my forearm as a brilliant smile spreads across her face.

Immediately, cameras flash from the paparazzi covering the charity gala for local society papers and websites to national and international media outlets. They call Signy's name since she's a regular on the social scene.

She alights from the Bentley with grace. Her gown flows behind her as I escort her down the red carpet. She's a beauty amidst the other patrons lined up for photos or chatting with the camera crews. We pause in front of the step and repeat where the Larson Enterprises, Inc. logo blazes behind her. She smiles and points at it with a red-polished, manicured fingernail. The paparazzi go wild. The flashes blinding. I stand aside and respond to emails on my mobile.

A tug on my arm alerts me to Signy's return to my side. I smile, and we head inside for the rooftop ballroom with an outdoor terrace. The night goes as planned. We mingle with others during the cocktail hour. Females know better than to approach me with Signy on my arm. Her eyes flash if they come anywhere near me. I send my thanks to Viggo.

After my speech and dinner, Signy wants to get some air. Although I think she has her eye on a particular human male. Like I'll let that happen. But again, I indulge her.

We step through the opening created by the wall of glass sliding into side pockets. Others have the same idea of getting air, creating a crowd of designer gowns and tuxedos with laughter and the buzz of conversations all around. I glance at my Patek Philippe timepiece. Another thirty minutes, and we're out. I let Signy guide me in the direction the male took.

I stop, stunned.

Eyes narrow. Nostrils flare. Cock thickens. A rumble grows in my chest. The urge to howl grips my throat. I inhale deeply.

Carried on the breeze across the rooftop, the faint scent of cinnamon sugar caramel apples wafts towards me. The unique scent I inhaled as my first breath when born tantalizes my senses. The scent of the only she-wolf destined for me.

My fated mate.

~

Click the Image Below or Visit books2read.com/u/ bOnYo0 For Your Copy

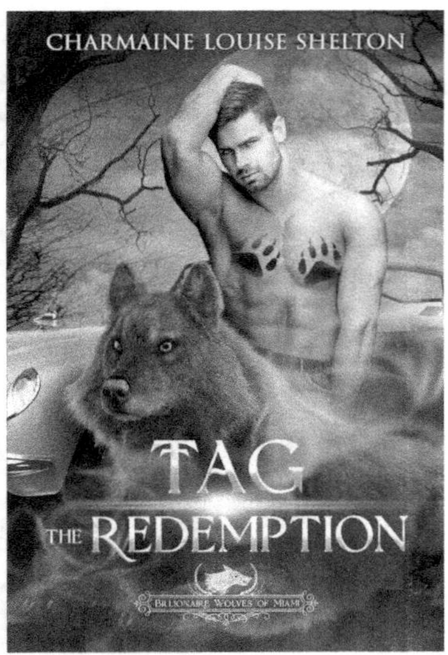

Tag The Redemption: A Wolf Shifter Fated Mates
Paranormal Romance

WANT FREE BOOKS?

Want to know what happened to Jagger's best friend Dylan? Find out in *Dylan The Rogue: A Wolf Shifter Fated Mates Paranormal Romance* **your FREE Book!**

Click Cover Below or visit **bit.ly/ CLBooksDylanTheRogue** to subscribe to my newsletter for latest news and launches, books from my author friends, and sizzling reads in book promotions. Plus, start reading the steamy fated mates romance for bad boy wolf shifter Dylan.

A Trilogy of Desires Roger & Leonie Parts I-III

Series Extras

Series Playlist

STEELE INTERNATIONAL, INC. - JACKSON
CORPORATION
A BILLIONAIRES ROMANCE SERIES CROSSOVER

Tempt My Desires Lachlan & Haley Part I

Tease My Desires Lachlan & Haley Part I

Grant My Desires Lachlan & Haley Part III

JACKSON CORPORATION

A BILLIONAIRES ROMANCE SERIES

Evoke My Desires Laurent & Yessenia Prequel

Light My Desires Laurent & Yessenia Part I

BILLIONAIRE WOLVES SERIES

WOLF SHIFTER FATED MATES PARANORMAL ROMANCE

MIAMI

Jagger The Awakening

(Available Exclusively for a Limited Time in Lunar Rising: A
Collection of Paranormal Romance)

Dylan The Rogue

(Available Exclusively to Subscribers)

Jagger The Temptation

Rust The Rejected

Tag The Redemption

Viggo The Obsession

ABOUT CHARMAINE LOUISE SHELTON

Charmaine Louise Shelton loves a dominant Alpha hero—human, shifter, or vampire—as long as he's a billionaire and sexy as sin! Her romance novels take readers into the heroes' glitzy, glamorous, steamy worlds as they chase after independent women who unexpectedly capture their hearts. Want to experience some more? Download a free book at CharmaineLouiseBooks.com!

Find her at:

CharmaineLouiseBooks.com

Follow her on social media on your favorite channels below and **download your Free Book** at CharmaineLouise Books.com.

Fulfill Your Desires.

9 781956 804249